A DEAD RED MIRACLE

Happy Reading

by RP Dahlke

RP Dahlke

A Dead Red Miracle
© 2015 RP Dahlke. vs 10.7.15
Published in the USA by Dead Bear Publishing

CREDITS

Editors: Ruth Ann Hixon, Asa Stephens, Beth Lake: http://createinput.com

Beta Readers and BFFs: Beth Englehart, Victoria Trout, Jennifer Wing, Lisa Cox, Gail Hall, Debby Kelly, Vickie Bolton, Joy Hart, Nancy Silk, Sandy Tucker and Sherry Wells

Experts: Mike McKearney, Fry District Fire Chief, Douglas Graeme, Queen Mine Tour Manager, Cochise County Search and Rescue member Evonne Ohlenzen

Cover Art: Karen Phillips-email: kphillips101@ymail.com

Formatting: Deb Lewis: arenapublishing.org

DEDICATIONS

*To my darling daughter, Dettre Galvan,
my beautiful granddaughters, Simone and Hanna
Shanahan, and to my husband, Lutz Dahlke for his
patience with all the hours I've put into writing.
Don't worry, honey, dinner will be ready when the smoke
alarm goes off!*

Chapter One:

With summer monsoons gusting wind and rain on my head, I opted for our cranky elevator to the second floor, backed through the wedged open door to 202A, *Ron Barbour Investigations*, and laid the box of printer paper on the nearest desk.

Shaking water from my windbreaker, I tossed it over the skeleton hanging on its stand in the corner.

The skeleton was a prop meant to help us ascertain where the knife, bullet, or hammer could strike. Another one of Ron's jokes since cousin Pearlie and I had yet to see a murder case come through the door. We worked for divorce attorneys, and insurance companies who needed proof against those people who made scamming a career choice.

Pearlie was hunched over a styrofoam head on her desk. I flopped into the vacant chair next to her desk. "Studying wound entries again?"

She looked up, boredom dulling her normally bright blue contact enhanced eyes. "Huh?"

"Never mind. Where's Ron?"

She went back to examining the head. "Ron who?"

"Ron Barbour, our fearless leader?"

She glanced at her watch. "He *said* he was going to see about drumming up some business. But since it's almost noon, he's probably cozied up to a beer."

"You should be grateful," I said. "It could be worse, you know."

Pearlie snorted. "Yeah. He could be trying for a three-some again."

I was thinking more of the times he came reeling through the door, slamming into furniture and reeking of whiskey. Ron was not a happy drunk, and since surly, belligerent and argumentative was not something we enjoyed with our workday, Pearlie and I tended not to question his daily routine.

She held up the styrofoam head for my inspection. "What do you think?"

"That depends. What is it?"

"A cap. Rather stylish, don't you think? I made it out of paper clips."

"Looks more like a contraption for torture. Don't you have anything to do?"

She grunted something that sounded like an expletive.

Technically, Pearlie and I owned the business, but because the State of Arizona required at least three years of documented experience in either state, federal police or military police, or as interns to a licensed P.I., we chose door number three. But getting anyone to accept us as interns was harder than we thought. We were over thirty, we had none of the aforementioned experience, and we were blonde. That last strike was incredibly sexist and so very annoying, but we soon realized that the best way to crack this nut was to buy into an established business. That's when Pearlie found Ron Barbour's ad in a P.I. magazine.

Our first phone call ended with Ron hanging up on Pearlie. At her second call and before he hung up on her again, he asked which of his friends put her up to this nonsense. At her third and final phone call, he reluctantly agreed to meet with us. Pearlie, never one to be fooled by a sales job done to impress, had done her homework. She knew what his business was worth and how much we should pay for it. A checkbook, a contract, and a pen nudged the grin off Ron Barbour's face.

Pearlie's airtight contract gave Ron one half of his asking price at signing, splitting expenses and profit during our time as interns, and at the end of the contract, he would write up letters of recommendation on our behalf as private investigators to the State Licensing Board and he would retire to go fishing.

We got the nominal title of *Associate* printed on our business cards, but not on the door or in ads. We did the grunt work, wrote up and initialed reports, and with Ron's signature, an invoice went to the client and checks came in made out to *Ron Barbour Investigations.* There was no mention of his silent partners, Pearlie or Lalla Bains, but since we were now a Limited Liability Corporation, there were now three signatures at the bank. Ron remained as titular big cheese, Pearlie became the company accountant handling all bank transactions, deposits, expenses, and taxes, and I did what I always wanted to do, work all day, every day as an investigator.

But before the ink was dry, Ron showed us in his own inimitable way that he regretted selling out to a couple of *dumb blondes*.

When Pearlie asked what we should do for desks, Ron leered and waggled his eyebrows. "Babe, as long as I have a face, you have a place to sit."

Actually, *Babe* became our unofficial titles. But when Pearlie and I started calling him *dickhead* in front of his clients, he called a truce.

That lasted for a month until he stopped bathing, shaving, or changing clothes. By this time, we were on to his antics and simply cranked up the A/C.

Next, he proposed a three-way at his place after work. Pearlie and I burst out laughing, then laughed again as his face turned beet red with humiliation. When he shouted and stamped his foot in fury at our insubordination, we pointed and laughed at his silly behavior. When he turned on his heel and stomped out of the office, we collapsed onto our chairs, gleefully giggling, and high-fiving each other in triumph.

In revenge, he had us doing every dirty, disgusting dumpster dive, all-night surveillance, and every boring fact-finding mission he could throw at us. In the process, we learned how to squeeze free information out of public records, credit bureaus, title searches, and social media. Tightwad that he was, we had to buy our own digital cameras and long distant lenses. He did let us use the beater Fords he kept for surveillance, but only if we bought our own gas. He also taught us how to mark a cheating spouse's tire at a no-tell-motel so we could come back the next morning, photo the mark on the tire, time and date it to show that the car hadn't moved all night.

And he never, ever, quit reminding us that under no circumstances were we to tell anyone of our partnership. If the clients found out he was retiring anytime soon, he'd said, they'd desert like rats fleeing the plague.

Oddly, this year's business was sliding faster than a monkey on a stripper's pole. One insurance company moved its local office out of state, another decided to accept a cheaper offer, and yet another simply went out of business. Ron seemed to spend a lot of his lunches looking for more work, and I smelled a rat. Maybe now was a good time to bring my suspicions to Pearlie.

"Last week," I said, "I presented a report to one of our clients and he asked who he should make the check out to."

"You're tired of having checks made out to Ron Barbour Investigations? Me too."

"Pearlie, I'm beginning to think..."

"You think buying this guy's business wasn't such a good idea? You read my mind. And to think, only a few months ago, the phone was ringing off the hook."

"Yes," I said. "Odd that Ron's client list is drying up right when we're less than a month away from giving him his final twenty-thousand dollar check and getting our letter of recommendation to the state."

Pearlie blinked. *Was she beginning to see the light?*

"I was at the court this morning. A woman was arrested for shooting her husband looked promising. She got bail, but her brother elbowed me aside and announced he'd hired a *man* for the job. I don't know how she could accept a man when it was obvious the case needed me."

"Us," I said, reminding her that we were partners. I wasn't about to let her forget, since this deal was *her* idea.

"Yeah, us, but I'm easy to talk to, you know."

"Because you're short?" Now I was teasing. The difference in our heights always got a rise out of her.

"I think it's because I'm not a threat to women," she sniffed, "on account of being a normal-sized female."

Got to hand it to her, she never missed a chance to remind me that I'm the beanpole. I'm tall and blonde, and she's short, plump, and blonde; at least she is when she makes it to her hair appointments on time.

Pearlie looked around the room as if seeing it for the first time. "Maybe Ron was right, maybe women P.I.'s don't do as well as men."

This was new. Of the two of us, Pearlie hung onto the dream of having our own P.I. firm with the clenched jaw of a pit bull. "You *are* depressed. You'll feel better after lunch," I said, knowing Pearlie could be easily distracted by food.

She smiled, pushed out of her fake leather executive chair and grabbed her purse. "I hope you're buying; I'm almost broke."

When it came to money, Pearlie Mae Bains would be the last person to be truly broke. Still, she hated the thought that her bank account had dipped below the water line with no prospects of a refill. Someone was going to have to hit Ron's list of old clients or we were going to be starting our new business with two dollars in our account.

"Of course I'm buying," I said, opening the door.

Pearlie's face lit up and I gathered that there was either a pizza delivery or a good looking man standing on the other side.

He wasn't wearing UPS brown or holding a pizza box, so maybe this was a potential client.

He was about five-nine, early twenties, with coppery muscled skin and the distinctive epicanthic fold of a Native American.

I smiled and motioned him inside.

With only a nod to acknowledge the two of us, he strode into the office taking in the shabby furniture, the dim overhead fluorescent lighting and the ancient file cabinets behind the WWII issue metal desk. "Where's Mr. Barbour?" he demanded.

"Pearl Mae Bains," she said, pumping his hand. "And this is Lalla Bains. We're Ron Barbour's associates. How can we help you?"

The young man pulled his hand out of hers and said, "If you don't mind, I'll take it up with Ron."

The kid wasn't exactly rude, but he sure was single minded.

Pearlie had that perplexed look. The one that meant that her clever mind had snagged on a thought. I could only hope it was the same one I'd been considering. I waited, studying a corner of the office while she worked it through to its ugly conclusion.

Her blue eyes darkened and her mouth went tight. Yep. She's seeing it now. Here was a real, live paying client, standing right in front of us. Just not one we knew about.

"I'm sorry," she said, her sweet sounding words belying the tight line of her mouth. "He retired and we bought his business."

The young man's eyes widened. "Retired! But he just called me."

"He called you *today*?" she asked, fluttering lashes that could cut glass. "He must've forgotten, on account of being in a hurry to leave. But we have all his files. If you'll just give me your name, Mister…?"

He shoved his hands in his pockets and glared at Pearlie. "Sorry, but I'm not talking to a couple of associates."

Pearlie lifted her chin and pulled herself up to her full five-foot three inches. "Well then I'm sorry for you, buster, 'cause if you want that information, you're gonna have to talk to *us*."

He shuffled from one foot to the other, and said, "I was training in the mountains and didn't get his message until today. He said he had a name and I have his check," he said, waving the check at us. "I called him back but it went to voice mail. If you're his associates, how come you didn't answer the phone?"

Pearlie and I looked at each other. Ron was giving out his cell phone for new business? We were going to have to talk to him about this.

Seeing Pearlie's hair trigger temper was about to let go, I pushed in front of her. "If you couldn't reach him, it's because you were calling his cell, not the office. He handed over the keys, and said he was going fishing."

"Did he say where?" the kid asked, desperation causing his voice to raise an octave.

"Sorry, no," Pearlie replied. "But like I told you, we own the business and we're certainly capable of handling your case."

"This is just wrong. Why would he call and then run off like that? A name—all I need is a name."

I thought it more likely that Ron Barbour had found a gullible client.

Seeing that the kid was waffling, she tried nudging again. "You can help by telling us the case name, or your name."

We held our breath, waiting to see if he would bite.

The kid, however, wasn't interested in our explanations. "You tell him he'd better call me or the deal's off!"

And before Pearlie could make a grab for the check, he turned on his heel and left, the door slamming shut behind him.

"That went well," I said. "Lunch?"

"That lazy, good fer nothin', lyin'... that sleaze bag Ron." Pearlie's face was flushed and there were tears in her eyes. "He's been hidin' cases from us!"

"The thought had crossed my mind." I was tempted to say I-told-you-so, but if I waited, Dad, Caleb, and Aunt Mae would do it for me.

Pearlie wiped away a tear, and tossing her purse on the desk, went to the file cabinet. "I'm going to look for this guy's files."

"Pearlie," I said, laying a gentle hand on her shoulder. "I know it's hard to take, but if Ron's been siphoning off clients, he's got the file with him."

Pearlie rounded on me. "Then let's saddle up and go find that polecat."

She was right. It was time for a showdown with Ron. "As long as you promise to leave your Pearlie special in the car!" I called after her as she clattered down the wet metal stairs.

"Sure," she said. "Who needs a gun when I can strangle him with my bare hands!"

A nondescript beige sedan sat in her parking spot.

"What's this?" I asked.

"Tight-ass Ron wouldn't let me borrow one of his precious surveillance vehicles while Gypsy gets her oil changed, so I had to rent a car."

Pearlie saw her move to Arizona as an opportunity to tour around her adopted state. But since most of our work was in Tucson, the miles she would've spent touring in her nice new Jeep Grand Cherokee were racked up in miles on the job, and it was beginning to show.

"Get in," Pearlie said, through clenched teeth.

I got into the rental car and sniffed. "Is it just me, or does this car smell like cat piss?"

Instead of answering, she turned on the radio and started flipping channels. "Why is it that all we get is Country Western or Mexican stations?"

"In case you haven't noticed," I said, "Sierra Vista is spitting distance from the Mexican border. So, let me guess–the local agency heard about your reputation for breaking rental cars?"

"Now you're just picking on me."

"Admit it. Your track record has caught up with you."

"Fresno was *not* my fault. You were there. It was a hit and run."

"If the perp had stuck around, you might've had a case."

Pearlie gave me a satisfied nod. "That's one less killer the feds have to worry about. He's just lucky my aim was off that day or he'd be pushing up daisies instead of sitting in prison."

"I'm sure he thanks you in his prayers."

"Ha-ha. As for rental car companies, I'm sick and tired of them. Soon's I get some money, I'm going to buy me a nice big truck."

"You have the Jeep."

"I don't want to get it messed up," she said.

I laughed. "Of course not. Sure you don't want a Hummer? They can take a beating."

"They cost a fortune. Besides, we have to keep a low profile. Ron always says a vehicle common to the area, something neutral, like a white or grey sedan."

"You're going to have to stop talking about Ron Barbour or I'm going to vomit on your cat-piss smelling seat covers."

"I know," she said, her voice going soft. "He's a rotten bastard, but he does have some redeeming qualities."

"You mean besides stealing our clients? If he's stealing clients, he might as well skip out on writing that letter of recommendation to the state for us."

"Ohmygod. I think I must be depressed or sumpin'."

More than likely, she was hungry again, but food was going to have to wait. I did not envy Ron when my cousin finally got him by the throat.

~~~~~~~~~~~

He wasn't at any of his favorite haunts so we decided to try the address we had for his house. It wasn't like Ron ever invited us over for holidays, but still we were surprised by the rundown neighborhood. Shingles were missing from roofs, homes hadn't been painted since the Nixon administration, and weeds fought for space in the gravel.

Pearlie slowly passed each house until she stopped in front of a rusty mailbox with the number 1642 on it.

We gawked at the derelict condition of the home.

"I can't believe he'd park his Lexus in that carport," I said.

"This is the right house number," Pearlie said, opening the car door. "I'd knock on doors and ask, but there doesn't appear to be anyone at home."

"Too bad," I said. "I was looking forward to watching you charm the neighbors, 'cause you're so easy to talk to."

The damp sky only added to our bad mood. I should be glad for the monsoon weather; it acted as a natural water cooler to the dry Arizona climate. But dishonesty and betrayal had left me hot anyway. I shrugged off my anger at Ron and considered the house he claimed to be living in. None of the other houses on the street were in such bad shape. At the very least it looked neglected, and it only added to my suspicion that he'd given us a fake address.

Pearlie opened Ron's mailbox and slammed it shut. "The resident spider inside said Ron doesn't get his mail here. Bet you five dollars it all goes to a P.O. box, the rat bastard."

"Are you getting the picture now?"

Pearlie ignored the comment, marched to Ron's front door and rapped three times. When no one answered, she leaned on the doorbell. "He's probably sleeping off his lunch."

I sidestepped to a living room window, cupped my hands against the glass, and peered inside. There was a fat bald man sprawled out on the floor, and though his face was turned away, I thought he looked a lot like Ron.

Was that dust in the air?

No. Not dust. It was… Smoke!

Hot, swirling, angry smoke crawled across the motionless body on the floor and curled up onto the windowsill.

I stumbled back, grabbed Pearlie's hand, and jerked her off the porch just seconds before the windows exploded, the blast knocking us face down into the gravel of Ron's front yard.

Window glass rocketed over our heads and heat scorched our backs, leaving us gasping.

When the searing heat subsided enough for me to raise my head, I looked up and saw that the house was fully engulfed in flames.

My face hurt from being tossed onto the gravel, and my ears were ringing, but I struggled to my feet, and pulled Pearlie with me to safety.

At the wail of sirens in the distance, Pearlie coughed and said, "Well that didn't take long."

Yep. My lucky streak was over.

Chapter Two:

Firemen with axes and hoses poured out of their trucks and rushed to the house. I didn't envy them the job. Flames came in waves from the broken windows and a hole in the roof to swirl into the sky and mix with rain-filled clouds.

Satisfied that Pearlie and I weren't going to need a ride to the hospital, the EMTs removed pieces of glass from our skin, bandaged the scrapes on elbows, knees and faces, and left us to give aid elsewhere.

A man in a dark, neatly pressed suit and tie, cell phone to his ear, got out of his unmarked police car and strode toward us.

Pearlie, noting the man's confident stride, said, "Whadya think—Homicide?"

"Probably," I said with a sigh. "Almost three years under our belts with no murders attached to our names, and now this. I don't know what I'm going to tell Caleb. You got soot on your face."

"Wasn't our fault Ron's house went up in smoke," she said, reaching up to wipe at the soot with her sleeve.

The detective's sharp brown eyes swept over us. Hair singed, soot clinging to our clothes, smeared makeup, a piece of tape here and there—not our most professional look.

When his lips dared to twitch, Pearlie's lip curled into a snarl. "Something funny, Detective?"

He had the audacity to smile. "I'm Detective Hutton, and you are?"

"Pearlie Mae Bains," Pearlie said, daring him to accept her dirty hand to shake.

A dimple appeared in the detective's cheek and just as quickly disappeared.

"I see you've been checked over by the EMTs," he said, wiping the soot from his right hand with a clean, folded hankie.

Pearlie grinned at the fastidious behavior. "A little singed around the edges is all."

When he ducked his head to write in his notebook, Pearlie snickered, "Tight ass."

I nudged her to keep quiet. We had enough trouble for one day.

When he looked up again, Pearlie's expression was blandly impersonal, but unless I had missed the signals, she had caught the detective's fancy.

"What can you tell me about the fire?" he asked, trying to keep the dimple in check.

I figured now was as good a time as ever and said, "I saw a man on the floor through the living room window."

Pearlie's blue eyes rounded in horror. "What? Y'all didn't tell me there was a body in that house!"

Anger and fear brought out the Texas in my cousin.

"That's because I was too busy trying to pry you off the porch before the house exploded."

The detective's earlier amusement quickly disappeared. "What made you think the house was going to explode?"

Jeez, just because we're blonde, he thinks we're dumb? I explained. "It's a small house. I could see the oven door in the kitchen hanging open. Couple that with a body on the floor, and I think it's a pretty good guess that someone had turned the gas oven on high. The electric doorbell could've acted as ignition, or someone had set an incendiary device to go off."

"The body… it could be Ron Barbour," Pearlie said, swallowing hard. "It's his house."

The detective's pencil stopped working its way across the pad. "Ron Barbour, the P.I.?"

The way he said it made me think the detective wasn't a fan of Ron's. *Get in line, bub.*

"We were here to ask him about one of our cases," I said.

"You worked for him?"

Pearlie, unable to keep the sour note out of her voice, said, "We're his *partners.*"

"Oh?" he said, now interested.

I elbowed her aside. "Technically, we own Ron's business."

"Except no one exactly knew it but us," Pearlie added.

"Is that so," he said conversationally. He twirled the pencil between two fingers looking from Pearlie to me. Was he waiting for one of us to blurt something that might prove we were a couple of firebugs? *Good luck with that, Detective.*

"The case needed some clarification," I said, glancing at the sagging roof, the broken windows, the missing front door and the milling crowd behind the fire trucks gathered to watch the firefighters tamp out the last of Ron's Barbour's destroyed house. "We thought we should talk to him in person."

"Uh-huh." His eyes roamed over Pearlie then reluctantly let go.

"Which one of you is Chief Stone's wife?"

Pearlie inspected her dirty nails.

"That would be me," I said cheerfully. I could only hope that verifying my status as police chief Caleb Stone's wife might carry some weight with the detective.

His expression relaxed. Glad to see that Pearlie wasn't married? "Mrs. Stone—" he began.

"I use my maiden name, Detective. It's Bains, Lalla Bains."

He nodded, the dimple back in his cheek. "Being partners with Mr. Barbour, I'm sure you know the drill."

Pearlie sighed. "I'd like a shower first, if you don't mind."

He handed out cards, gave us a time to meet at the police station, then looking directly at my cousin. "Can I give either of you a ride?"

"We have a car," Pearlie said, and without meeting his gaze, put the card in her purse and snapped it shut.

The detective took the rejection with the good humor he was born with and left.

"Give us a ride, my ass," Pearlie said, watching him walk away.

"He *likes* you," I said, unable to keep from laughing. Soot covered, scrapes and all, Pearlie had made a conquest.

"Humph. He can *like* all he wants. Won't do him any good. Besides, he looks like a cover hog. Now what?"

"Now we talk to the fire chief and see what he'll tell us about the body on the floor in Ron's house."

I followed her to where yellow crime scene tape had been wrapped around the perimeter.

Pearlie flashed her P.I. card at a patrolman standing in her way. "We'd like to talk to the fire chief."

The patrol officer looked her up and down, a smile gathering at his lips. "Give me your card and I'll be sure he gets it."

Pearlie rolled her eyes and took out her notebook, pen scratching hastily on the pad. "Never mind," she said, peering at his name tag. "I'll tell him when I see him tonight at Chief Stone's house, *Officer* Nolan."

The patrolman snickered and gave her an abbreviated salute. "You do that, ma'am. And in the meantime I'll do my duty. No civilians allowed, even if they are pretty little blondes."

Annoyed, Pearlie returned the salute with a middle digit.

I pulled her away before the patrolman could take exception to the rude gesture.

"You're not helping," I said.

"Sorry. I'm so used to flipping off Ron that it's become a habit."

"Not everyone is Ron Barbour. Besides, that explosion was no accident."

"I suppose not. We weren't supposed to be here to witness it, either. Darn it. All I wanted to do was talk to him," Pearlie said, sniffling.

"You feel bad for Ron already?" I asked, heading for her rental car.

"No. I'm talking about the fire chief. If it turns out that wasn't Ron in there, I'm gonna kick his ass all the way to New York City."

"You'll have to get in line. A dead Ron is really going to complicate things."

Complicated didn't begin to describe the hornet's nest of trouble Ron's two ex-wives were going to cause, both of them in an uproar over their discontinued alimony checks.

Seeing Caleb's police cruiser pull up behind the line-up of EMT and fire trucks, Pearlie started backing away. "Um,

I gotta get a shower and see about getting a new rental. This one has dents in it."

She was leaving me to explain the fire and the dead body to Caleb. Can't say I blamed her. I'd skip out on this too, if I weren't married to Wishbone's police chief.

Caleb's ice blue eyes took in the smoldering ruin of Ron Barbour's house, the scrapes, the soot on my face, and the weeds sticking out of my hair.

"How do you do it, Lalla? Last time we spoke you were on your way to see how your dad's new patio was coming along. What the hell happened this time?"

"Pearlie… "

"I knew she was going to be trouble."

"Now, Caleb, that's just not fair. We were looking for our *business partner*." I sighed again. Pearlie had me doing it. My heart sank at what we would lose if that body turned out to be Ron.

"The detective I just talked to seemed to think you found him, too."

"About that… "

The fire chief interrupted our argument. "Hello, Caleb. This your missus?" he asked, shaking hands with Caleb.

Caleb introduced me to the chief.

"What can you tell us, Chief McKerney?" Caleb asked.

The chief confirmed my initial theory about the gas oven and a probable incendiary device, but added, "Things like this can work, or not. It all depends on the right mix of oxygen and gas."

"Is-is the body I saw through the window Ron Barbour?" I asked.

The chief's appraisal of me was not entirely unfriendly. "That'll have to be determined by the medical examiner. I heard you were in the process of buying him out."

"If you heard that, then you're the only one."

Chief McKerney smiled broadly. "If it's any consolation, Ron said you two came with ready-made disguises."

"That's our Ron," I said, lightly. "Always good for another dumb blonde joke."

"We'll get confirmation on identity with his dental records and I'll have someone let you know as soon as possible."

Caleb thanked the fire chief for the update and then silently steered me toward his cruiser. "I'm on my lunch break, so you can tell me exactly what happened while I drive you home."

His voice was calm but it had an edge to it that said we were going to have one of those talks about my reckless behavior.

Ah, there it was. That familiar feeling I'd been missing—me in trouble again.

Chapter Three:

Caleb and I never intended to marry in Arizona. We had a simple fall wedding planned for friends and family at Roxanne's café in Modesto, California. But when Caleb interrupted a robbery at a Quick Stop it was inevitable that he should be the one to cuff the thief until the city police arrived. The good news was that he got a reprieve on the paperwork. The bad news was that I had jumped to my usual erroneous conclusion that he would be a no-show, and dumping my wedding bouquet, I fled to Arizona, taking my dad with me on an ill-advised road trip.

Caleb, knowing me as he did, wasn't about to let me run off without an explanation. That his truck was hijacked and he was left to wander in the desert until he made it back to town only served to prove that it wasn't Caleb who had the cold feet.

When we finally did get married, we moved into the old federal style adobe house gifted to us as a wedding present by my great-aunt Eula Mae Bains. Because we wanted to keep the integrity of the historic home, we kept the windows and French doors, but redid the plumbing to accommodate a dishwasher in the kitchen, and carved out a laundry room from what had been a perfectly nice second bedroom. It was small, but then it was only Caleb and me. And though he was here for dinner more often than not, my dad and his dog Hoover, lived on forty acres adjoining our property.

Hoover, the stray my dad had adopted was so named because he ate everything, including an occasional wayward sock, and we now worked as volunteers with Cochise County's Search and Rescue as an air scent dog and handler.

With Caleb's acceptance as Wishbone's police chief, and Pearlie and I working toward acquiring a business as private investigators, life was pretty good. It only took two years and seven months to be disabused of that idea.

I wrapped a towel on my wet hair, pulled on a terry cloth robe and went to the kitchen where Caleb had lunch waiting.

I don't know how many times I have asked that man not to feed Hoover anything but dog food, but there they were, Caleb handing down bites of tuna to the eager dog.

"Come on Caleb, you know I use treats to reward him for good work."

He shrugged and patted the dog between his big ears. "I'm training him, too."

"To beg?"

"Hoover is learning new tricks and that deserves a treat, doesn't it boy?" he said, patting Hoover on the head.

Hoover wagged his tail.

"What new tricks?"

Caleb smiled and said, "Hoover—play dead."

The dog promptly laid down, closed his eyes, and let his tongue hang out.

When I laughed, Hoover cracked open an eye and wagged his tail.

Caleb spoke softly and the delinquent eye shut and his tail went quiet.

"And this is useful how?"

"Watch," Caleb said, waving a dollop of tuna in front of the dog's nose.

The eyes stayed closed, the body limp, but there was that cheating tail thumping again.

"Needs some work," Caleb said, and withdrew the tuna. "Not sure where or when it might become useful, but I think it's a good trick."

"Just so long as he doesn't lie down and play dead on search and rescue."

Caleb smiled. "When does Hoover go out again?"

"When they need us," I said. "Karen's dog is still the veteran and first choice on the team, but if she's not available, it's up to Hoover."

"You sure he's capable?"

"Karen Paquette said he's as good as they come—even if he is a big baby when it rains. That dog hates the rain."

"I felt you come to bed late last night. How'd it go with finding those hikers?" he asked.

"Dumb kids. It's dark, they're lost, and since they're too smart to own a compass or bring along a GPS, they used their cell phone and called 9-1-1."

"I'm sure their mothers were glad they did," he said.

"Whose side are you on?"

"Yours, of course."

"So you say," I said, reaching over and pinching his arm. I had no problem putting off our talk about Ron, but when Caleb's cell phone rang, I hoped it was for an update on the house fire.

He held up a finger for me to wait. "Uh-huh. Yeah. I will, thanks." He hit the off button and pocketed the cell, watching me lift a corner of my tuna sandwich.

"You didn't add pickles to mine did you?" I asked.

"Oh, I remembered," he said, picking up half of his sandwich and leaning against the counter to eat.

I happily dug into mine, only to taste the pickle relish I so detested. "Caleb! What gives?"

Pointedly side-stepping pickles, he said, "I thought you would want to know about my morning. The usual vagrancy issues with the park and I released the drunks from last night's brawl on their own recognizance, then on my way out of town I caught the Garza brothers stealing a battery out of someone's car."

I decided to ignore my issue with pickles. "Those two again? They're eight and ten—why aren't they in school?"

"The older one was suspended for smoking and his little brother decided it would be more fun to take the day off and see what they could steal."

"Where does a ten-year-old get cigarettes? Oh, yeah, their mom. What'd she have to say this time?"

"On a good day we can find her at a local bar, but today she's gone AWOL."

"They have an older brother, don't they?"

"Step-brother. He works at the Shell station and says he's done with those two."

"Then they're headed for Juvie?"

"There's no one at home to watch them. If I hadn't come by when I did, they would've had that car stripped and the parts sold."

"Who teaches this kind of stuff to little kids?"

"Their uncle Carlos. He's locked up but what the boys really need is a different environment."

"They're just little boys. Isn't there anyone who can help?"

"Doesn't look like it. Not with an absent mother and an indifferent half-brother. Foster care will be the best we can hope for."

"They'll split them up won't they?"

"Those two feed each other trouble, so that might not be a bad thing. Look," he said, scratching at the back of his head, "If it helps, I'll call Sheriff Tom. Ask him to look into something for the boys."

"Why Sheriff Tom?"

"Because the mother is Chiricahua Apache and if you remember, Sheriff Tom is half Apache. Maybe he can find foster parents for the boys on the res."

"Well, that's something. Thanks, Caleb," I said. Though I wasn't sure how much the boys would thank anyone if they ended up on the res. I'd never been to the Chiricahua reservation, but our search and rescue team leader said it was like most reservations, too much alcohol, no prospects for jobs, and no chance for a child to grow up with any kind of hope of getting one.

Putting aside the subject of the Garza boys, now was as good a time as any to bring up Ron Barbour. "Did Sheriff Tom happen to have anything to say about the fire?"

"In a manner of speaking."

I took a bite of my sandwich and pretended to ignore the pickles. My husband thought unwanted pickles might remind me that I'd neglected to call him the minute I thought there might be trouble; like I should've known that Ron's house was going to blow up.

"Caleb," I said, pushing aside my plate and grabbing a handful of chips. "You know how hard Pearlie and I have worked for what we thought was going to be our very own P.I. firm. Yet, in the last months business has been falling off and yes, Ron had his excuses, but today a client showed up asking for him. A client we knew nothing about."

"He was retiring, anyway, why would he do that?"

"Hide income from his two greedy exes? Cheat his business partners? And as awful as it sounds, we're beginning to think this was all part of his escape plan. If we hadn't gone to his house for a showdown...."

"You think someone beat you to it?"

"Pearlie wanted to kill him. I just wanted to talk."

"You've never mentioned going to his home before today."

"We had enough of Ron every day without going to his home."

"I can find out who owns the house, but if he didn't live there then why do you think it was Ron on the floor?"

"I don't know, maybe three years of looking at his bald spot and bad suits? I'm pretty sure it was Ron."

"What about the kid and his case—he didn't give you a phone number so you could contact him?"

"No, and nothing in the files for any murder case, much less one with someone owing us money. All we had were the few insurance cases we were finishing up. Add insult to injury, our recommendation to the state for our P.I. license is now circling the drain."

"You had a month on your three year internship. So what're you two going to do? Find another P.I. to work with?"

The thought of starting over again made my my stomach turn over. We had tried all the P.I.'s in Tucson and got laughed out of their offices. Ron was our best chance for a business of our own and I couldn't let it go. Not now. Not after all the time and money we spent on this deal.

"I'll tell you what we're going to do; we're going to find Ron Barbour's killer and the name of the person that kid was looking for and the nice fat check for doing it right."

Even to my ears it sounded like so much hubris. But then, Ron Barbour was, if nothing else, a darn good investigator. And didn't he teach Pearlie and me everything we knew about investigating?

Chapter Four:

Leaving Caleb to clean up after lunch; I stopped by my dad's place to see how his helpers were doing on a new concrete walkway and a backyard patio. The young Mexican workers were leery of dogs, so Hoover had to take up residence with us, at least until the concrete was poured and cured. Unfortunately the truck was still waiting for a dry spell.

I was surprised to find my dad in a folding chair, a beer in one hand, a mining magazine in the other.

Looking over the half-finished foundation, I asked, "Did you get rained out again?"

"No rain, but they're finished for the day."

"Who quits at two in the afternoon?"

"Mexican holiday. Some saint's birthday or something."

"Uh-huh," I said, figuring Rafael and his two cousins had a soccer game. "Those boys trot out a new saint's day every week. Aren't you going into Wishbone today? You still have lunch with Cie Taylor, don't you?"

"Not if I can help it."

Though Dad would be the first to say there was nothing between him and the landlady who ran Wishbone's only B&B, everyone else knew Cie Taylor had plans for widower Noah Bains.

"Then what're you doing out here?" I asked.

"I'm waiting on my lunch and here it comes," he said, getting out of his chair and tucking in his shirt.

"Cie is bringing you lunch?"

"Not Cie, Rafael's aunt."

Knowing how much my dad missed our housekeeper from California and her Mexican meals, I could see how he would be interested in the aunt's cooking.

"That's nice of her. Does she live in Wishbone?"

"Douglas," he said, smiling.

I shaded my eyes with a hand and watched a white pickup trailing a cloud of dust turn into his driveway. "All the way from Douglas?"

"She's also looking for a housekeeping job."

I looked him up and down. "I thought you said you weren't interested in having another housekeeper."

Dad snorted and loped for the pickup. He held the door for her with one hand and took the covered dish with the other. Turning for the house, he was smiling again. Now, that was something. It must be the familiar fragrance of cumin and roasted peppers.

Her hair was completely covered with a scarf, and I could see that she was small. A tiny little thing and probably too old and frail to do housework, but hoping her cooking would tilt the scales in her favor.

Then she removed her scarf, releasing a cascade of shiny black hair. She reached up and pushed the bangs out of her eyes and I heard the tinkling sound of youthful laughter.

My father might be in his late sixties, but he was not immune to the flattery of a pretty woman and certainly not one who brought food. He waved her over to make the introductions.

"Lalla, this is Rafael's aunt, uh, what'd you say your name was again?"

In a patently flirtatious gesture, she tilted her chin to one shoulder and looked up at him through a pair of sparkling chocolate brown eyes.

"Oh, Señor Bains. I tol' you. I am Coco Lucero," she said, giving her words a breathy lisp.

Housekeeper? Coco Lucero looked like she should come with castanets and dancing shoes. B&B owner, Cie Taylor had better look out. Her competition just arrived.

~~~~~~~~~~

Pearlie and I were in the office going over strategy for our interview with Detective Hutton when the phone rang.

Pearlie pantomimed surprise, her eyes wide. "You think it's Ron calling to tell us it was all a joke?"

"Answer it," I growled.

She grabbed the receiver off its cradle.

"Detective Hutton," she said, with a smile in her voice. "No, no, we haven't forgotten. As long as there won't be water-boarding involved, we'll be there. You want to change it to five? Sure. No problem."

Pearlie stuck out her tongue at the phone. "We have an hour's reprieve."

"Maybe he'll have an ID on the body by then," I said.

"Or maybe he'll have enough to charge us with *murder*."

"Don't say that," I said. "Besides, he seems to like you."

"Unless he decides we're responsible for Ron's murder." She put her chin in her palm and sighed. "If we'd only gone to the police academy, we'd have a badge by now."

"You don't like uniforms."

"The buttons're in all the wrong places. Besides, we'd be the oldest female rookies in the history of Wishbone's police department," she said.

"You couldn't live on the pay," I said, and winced. "And I wouldn't *want* to."

Pearlie shuddered. "Can you imagine what kind of harassment we'd have to take?"

I groaned. "More blonde jokes than I want to hear in a lifetime."

She tapped a pink-tipped fingernail on the table. "We have a knack for this job and P.I. work means we can take the jobs we want and we get to wear disguises."

"You mean those tacky flowered housedresses and strollers? I keep forgetting what a glamorous job this is."

"All those witnesses were more willing to talk to pregnant women than some old bald guy with a bent nose."

She held up her forefinger about an inch apart from her thumb. "We're this close to our dream job and I'm not willing to give it up now."

"Who says we have to? We have all those cases with our initials on them, our pay stubs and our tax returns. Surely the state will take that into account."

Pearlie smiled. "You really want this job then?"

"Of course I do!"

"I was hoping you'd say that," she said. "Because, I'm afraid that detective is going to try to make a case against us. Think about it Lalla, Ron's business was going down the tubes and we were coming up on a final payment we didn't have."

"The only reason it's failing is because Ron has been hiding clients." I cringed. "All he has to do is look at our contract to see we had motive."

She shrugged. "Maybe he won't think of it. We've got a week. We can play two dumb blondes. Oh come on. How many times have we used it to our advantage?"

"But the police will think we're incompetent."

"Let 'em. It's only until we find Ron's killer and solve this case. Then no one will be able to doubt us."

Pearlie hated being called a dumb blonde even more than I did, yet it was our best disguise.

"How long do you think we got until the state pulls Ron's license?" Pearlie asked.

I bit at my lower lip. "It'll take a week for Ron's death certificate to get to them. It's Monday. We have a week before they shut us down."

"Well then, let's get to it," she said, slapping the desktop. "So what *do* you remember about the kid?"

"He said he was in training, and he had an athletic patch on his sleeve," I said, tapping the spot on my shoulder.

She snapped her fingers. "That's right. I remember seeing it too. It was a gold and purple patch. We'll find him at the gym where he's training."

Pearlie listed the selections. "There's the Cochise Health and Racquet Club, Power Zone Gym, Summit Fitness. All of these are for weight lifting and the logos don't quite look right." She squinted at the print on the page, then leaned back and rubbed her eyes. "I'm going to need reading glasses. Wait... look at this one...here it is."

I read aloud. "Muay Thai, boxing, cross-fit, and training for American Ninja Warrior—whatever that is. Got any ideas on how to get an owner to reveal a member's name and address?"

Pearlie held up a finger. "I have a card for that."

She reached for her card folder, worked the card she wanted out of its plastic sleeve and shoved it across the desk. "This will do. I'm a renowned independent journalist working for the San Francisco Examiner, doing a piece on athletes training in Arizona."

I scrutinized the name. "Didn't the San Francisco Examiner go out of business?"

"They're now online news, and if I need it, I have a friend who can vouch for me," she said, swiveling around in her desk chair to pick up her laptop. "So it'll look like we know what we're doing, let's see what we can find on this stuff. I'll take the American Ninja Warrior and you look up MMA. Research always makes me hungry. Will you go over to Jack in the Box and pick us up some burgers and fries?"

I added research to the growing list of things that made my cousin hungry, grabbed my purse and left to get her a hunger-stopper.

When I got back to the office, Pearlie leaned away from the computer screen and rubbed her eyes. "No need to look up MMA. He's training for the American Ninja Warrior contest."

"Why do you say that?"

"For one thing, five hundred thousand dollars to the winner and for another...." She got up and slid the vertical blinds open on our second story window. A neat hole had been punched out of the glass.

"They break into offices?" I asked.

"Not as a rule, but they do climb walls. If he doesn't win the competition, he can always get a job as a second story man."

"He must really want that name to jeopardize his chance at five hundred thousand dollars," I sighed. "Did you call the police?"

"And miss out on losing a client? Not a chance."

"The file cabinets aren't locked. What'd he take?"

"My cell phone."

"Your cell? I thought you kept it in your purse?"

"Not today. I was in such a hurry to confront Ron, I left it in my desk drawer."

"He was looking for Ron's phone number," I said.

"Fat lot of good it'll do him now. Ron's dead."

"If he was looking for Ron about the same time we were, we can check him off our non-existent list of suspects. Have you called the landlord about the break-in?"

"The deductible on our insurance is too high and we don't have the cash in the bank to pay for a new window."

It also might be a tad embarrassing to admit that she'd been outwitted by a wall climbing ninja.

"So," I said, rubbing my hands together in anticipation. "We go to this gym and pretend to be journalists and ask if there are any young men training for American Ninja Warrior, right?"

"That's the plan."

Chapter Five:

The local gym where we hoped to find a lead on our ninja thief had ten or so cars parked outside. Inside, young men and women shouted encouragement to a rope climber while others swung from hanging boards, and another ran a gauntlet of slippery rolling drums.

An older man sidled up to us, his toothy smile beaming. "Hello ladies. If you're looking to join one of our MMA classes, we have signups open for Tuesday evenings."

"Actually," Pearlie said, handing him her fake journalist's card. "I'm writing an article about training for America Ninja Warrior and if you have some time, I'd like to interview the owner and a few of the athletes."

His pupils became dollar signs. "Well, you came to the right place. Outside of Phoenix, we're Arizona's premier ANW training center. Our trainers are former finalists and our trainees dedicate every minute of their lives to this year's contest."

"All that just for the title of American Ninja Warrior?" I asked, wide-eyed.

The owner leaned in as if to add his big secret. "Five hundred thousand dollars to the winner and product contracts worth as much as a million dollars."

Pearlie whistled and wrote it down in her notepad.

"It's not an easy win, either. Hundreds wait in line for a chance to compete. Entrants are selected from try-outs in five cities across America."

"But isn't Sierra Vista a bit out of the way?" Pearlie asked.

"All the major city gyms are filled to capacity. Training for the title is the newest, hottest thing for athletes. Did you see last season? The ANW held a side competition teaming the best Americans against European challengers, none of whom had ever done any of these games. Europe sent their best rock climbers; Swiss, French, Italian and English, and they never hesitated, they just flew through that course. That the Americans barely beat them by a few points has been taken seriously by the American teams. Now all our training includes rock climbing in the Chiricahuas."

The man peered at Pearlie's notes. "So what kind of circulation will your article have?"

"I expect the feature will get picked up by Reuters, and with the popularity of the show, it's sure to go viral, maybe even get a spot on NBC or CBS. You mentioned training in the Chiricahua Mountains. It might really heighten reader interest if any of your participants were local, maybe even Native American?"

"Hey, yeah, we got a Chiricahua Apache. That's our claim to fame here in Cochise County, you know. America's two favorite Indians, Geronimo and Cochise lived in this part of Arizona. That would be something if an Apache like this kid won, wouldn't it?" He looked at her card. "The San Francisco Examiner, huh? Well, let me see if I can find him for you."

He stepped away to talk to one of the trainees.

"I don't know, Pearlie," I said. "Maybe we're wasting our time."

"Bet you five dollars, he's here," she said. My cousin hadn't been to Vegas in three years, not after investing her life's savings in Ron's business, but since gambling came second nature to Pearlie, I couldn't resist being the chump who always said, "You're on."

Searching the participants, the owner called to a young man. "Hey, Mike, you seen Damian?"

The guy called Mike pointed at a back door as a faded blue Ford pickup fishtailed out of the parking lot, tossing gravel and peeling rubber as the tires hit the highway.

The owner's jaw dropped. "Well, uh, he must have an emergency of some kind. Damian wouldn't want to miss out on an opportunity to get his name in the news."

Pearlie tapped her pencil on her notebook as she glanced my way. Damian had ID'd us. By now, he must've heard that Ron had been murdered and was distancing himself from us, the law, and whoever killed Ron.

"Sorry we missed your Apache," I said, "but we'll be happy to interview Mike instead."

"Oh, sure," the owner said, drawing the guy over to us. "Mike here is a two time finalist."

Mike, delighted to be the center of attention, listened to my pitch, eagerly nodding at the idea of an exclusive interview. "I was in the second round last year, but the warped wall got me. This season we've built our own. If I can get past the floating boards, the doorknob grasper and the jumping spider, I'll win that title for sure."

Head nodding, Pearlie scribbled, giving the young man her undivided attention. After one more boring detail, the owner mumbled something about paperwork and left us alone.

Pearlie felt my nudge and put away her notebook. "I *would* like to interview your friend, Damian. You know, for local color. Does he live around here?"

"Damian? Oh, yeah. But he'll have to wait in line for a chance to compete and most of the new guys bomb out in the first round. They only take ninety for the TV show and like I said, last season I made it to the finals so chances are your readers will see me before they see Damian."

"Then I'll want to do a follow up on you too. What's your phone number?"

Now pleased to have the journalist in his corner again, he eagerly recited the number.

Pearlie looked up from writing. "And before I forget, do you have Damian's phone number or where he lives?"

Mike's forehead wrinkled in dismay. Refuse to be helpful and blow off a possible feature in a big newspaper, or cooperate and get his name in print and maybe even on TV?

He scratched at the back of his neck and said, "Well, I know he's darn proud of his Apache heritage. We got nicknames, you know. He insisted we call him by his namesake, Geronimo. He's staying with his uncle, so I guess it's okay if I give you the number."

Leaving the gym, Pearlie nudged me and winked. "Five bucks. You can pay me later."

I always fall for it, and of course, I always lose.

Chapter Six:

Leaving the gym where we'd just missed cornering our wall climbing Apache, I read aloud the address to the uncle's home on King's Ranch Road. "If we kept going on Highway 92," I said, "you'd see the old Bible College campus where that religious group took over."

"Anyone still live there?"

"I hope not. The roof is falling in, window glass and doors are gone. Whatever is still standing has been boarded up to keep the local kids out."

The left turn onto King's Ranch road was so potholed, it threatened to shake the fillings out of our teeth.

"It'll go away if you drive faster," I said.

She picked up speed and the ride smoothed out. "All these homes out here and they can't get the county to fix the road?"

"County living is a double-edged sword. Winter and summer rain goes where it wants to on unpaved roads, leaving gullies deep enough to hide a Volkswagen. Just count your blessings it isn't raining or your cat-piss rental would be in serious trouble."

"You gotta respect the kind of wild-west attitude folks have living here," Pearlie said.

"Did you know that Arizona was the last territory to become a state in the contiguous United States?"

"I heard they were hold-outs to join the Union," Pearlie said. "Southerners don't hold with Yankees."

For a dyed-in-the-wool southerner like Pearlie, a state's position on the Civil War was the bellweather of their trustworthiness.

Pearlie changed the channel on the radio, finally getting a station with current pop music. I felt an eerie shiver when the song *Say Geronimo* by Shepard came on.

Pearlie slowed and took a right onto a private driveway marked with a house number. Fenced and cross-fenced, there were cows and horses in the pasture. We parked next to a nice looking single story ranch house, took the short walk to the house, and knocked.

A tall, muscular man in his forties, white denim shirt tucked into sleek, faded jeans answered the door. His black eyes flickered from Pearlie to me. But before I could say anything, Pearlie stuck out her hand. "Howdy, sir. I'm...."

He ignored Pearlie to shake my hand. "Sorry, I missed the wedding, Lalla. I had a family emergency. Pardon my manners, ladies. What can I do for you?"

"Sheriff Ian Tom," I said, "This is my cousin Pearlie Bains. I wish this were a social call, but do you have a nephew by the name of Damian?"

Ian Tom's hand reached up to rub at the back of his neck. "What's that boy done now?"

~~~~~~~~~~~

Ian Tom ushered Pearlie and me into his living room and offered cold drinks. It took me six months to learn that a beverage offered in this part of Arizona is one part hospitality and one part war against dehydration. At four to five thousand feet, no one wants visitors collapsing from dehydration or altitude sickness. "Water would be great," Pearlie said.

"Me too," I said, settling into one of his comfy club chairs.

The living room was tidy, photos in simple frames lined a rustic mesquite mantle, and lamps with pierced tin shades sat on polished mesquite end tables. The wood was polished, the carpets clean, but I knew Ian had been on his own since his wife died of cancer several years ago.

Pearlie's eyes swept the room, her brows rising in question. I forgot that Pearlie hadn't met Ian Tom. She'd been in the hospital from a rattlesnake bite during the investigation of a murder when we first got to Arizona so, until now, she didn't have any reason to meet him.

"I'll tell you later," I whispered.

Ian brought back our cold water and perched on the edge of the couch to hear what we had to say about his nephew.

"Ian," I said. "It's not anything to get the police involved in; at least—not yet it isn't. Damian's staying with you while he trains for the next American Ninja Warrior competition, right?"

"It seemed like a good idea at the time," Ian said, unclenching his hands. "Damian has been in and out of trouble over the years, but I thought he'd cleaned up his act. What's he done now?"

"He broke a window to get into our office," Pearlie said with a huff.

When Ian reached for his wallet, Pearlie held up a hand. "It was a second story window, Sheriff. He scaled the outside wall to get to it and used a diamond cutter to open the latch. If it weren't so embarrassing, I'd give him a medal for creativity, but he stole my cell phone and I'm gonna want it back."

"Your office—you mean Ron Barbour's office? Caleb told me you ladies were interning with him. I thought paying for Damian's training would be enough, but he can be single-minded. Did he take anything else?"

"What do you know about this case, Ian?"

Ian looked up at the ceiling and then at us. "His father was a member of a religious cult in Palominas. It was years ago, before your time and mine too. There was an altercation with the sheriff's department. Both sides had guns, shots were fired and Damian's father was shot in the back. No one knows who shot him, but my nephew is now determined to find the person who killed him."

I nodded. "Damian came to our office this morning because he said Ron called to say he had a name for him. Do you know anything about that call?"

Ian looked from me to Pearlie. "No, I don't. What time did my nephew show up at your office?"

"About ten. I doubt he had anything to do with Ron's house blowing up."

"But someone obviously did," Ian said.

Pearlie's brows went up. "If it makes you feel any better, Homicide would be more willing to think we had reason to kill Ron Barbour."

"It's a long story, Ian," I said, "but it has recently come to our attention that Ron's business practices could sully our own reputations."

"Damian didn't believe that we were in the dark about his case," Pearlie said. "So he waited until we left and broke into the office. When he couldn't find what he was looking for he took my cell phone. I suppose he thought we were keeping Ron's whereabouts a secret."

I suppose you've told Homicide all this?" Ian asked.

I saw Pearlie thoughtfully consider before she answered. "We thought we'd talk to you first," she said.

Ian Tom bit at the inside of his cheek. "Thank you. I'll call Detective Hutton and make an appointment for Damian. He's over eighteen, but he has his mother's temper and impetuous nature, so I'll have to make sure he has a lawyer present for the interview. That is if he comes home at all."

"Has it been confirmed then?" Pearlie asked, glancing at me. "It was Ron Barbour in the house?"

"Yes. I got the news an hour ago. His dental records were with a local dentist. Homicide will release it for the news people right after they get in touch with next of kin."

"He had two ex-wives," I said.

Pearlie shot me a bitter smile.

I shrugged. Sooner or later Ron's exes would come sniffing around, looking for any crumbs he might have left on the table. Our final payment to him would become a bone of contention sooner than I would like, but I wasn't going to think about that now.

"Ron Barbour wasn't held in the highest regard in this county," Ian said.

"We've heard a few things," I said.

"It's not surprising that he would exploit a naïve kid like Damian," Pearlie said. Her sympathetic words countered my own growing suspicion that Ian might know more about Ron than he was saying. Was he protecting his nephew or someone else?

Ian flashed a quick and insincere smile. Her ploy wasn't going to work on him. He had, after all, been a homicide detective in Chicago before he came home to Arizona to work with the sheriff's department. "Please understand that I'm not unsympathetic to my nephew's search for justice," he said. "I had a serious look at the case before Damian took it on himself to hire a P.I. If for no other reason than to satisfy myself that everything had been done that could be done. I have to say that the entire file had little or no evidence collected, and the rest of it was just so much sloppy paperwork. It would never have been tolerated on my watch, that's for sure, but it was before my time."

"Was there any evidence on the shooter?" I asked.

"First, let me give you some background on Miracle Faith Church. Mahala Beason was a self-proclaimed messiah for people of color and anyone who felt disenfranchised. Setting herself up as the voice of God, she started calling herself Mother Beason and moved the group to Palominas in the hopes of taking over A.A. Allen's old bible college. When the sale didn't happen; she bought land across the highway and then began a vicious campaign against anyone who didn't go along with her doctrines. Naturally, trouble started when she closed ranks against the locals and white people. There were rumors of intimidation and corporal punishment within the congregation, but none of it could ever be confirmed. Some of the parishioners left with the help of a local church. Some worked in town and did fine, others got in trouble and arrests were made for everything from traffic violations to petty crime. The file I read said that warrants were issued for non-appearances at court, but the straw that broke the camel's back, so to speak, was when Mother Beason decided to put up a roadblock on Highway 92, effectively turning around all through traffic. It should've brought in the state police, but it looks like the governor thought it too political for the state troopers to handle so the local sheriff's department got the job.

"Deputies were sent with instructions to remove the barricades and arrest the miscreants. They were met by

Mother Beason and her church, armed and ready for battle. Knowing how badly this whole affair was handled, it's no surprise that there was nothing to prove, no slug found, or that no one was willing to testify as to who shot one of the rioters in the back."

"What happened after that?" I asked.

"As a church, Mother Beason was the cohesive link, and after the gunfight, she and her congregation deserted the property and never returned."

"Where did Damian get the money to pay for a private detective?" Pearlie asked.

"If Damian hired Ron Barbour, it was with his mother's blessing and *her* money. His mother, Naomi, is my sister. She makes a good living from her Apache jewelry and design. I just wish she didn't feel the need to fuel Damian's misdirected anger."

I had more questions about Damian's mother, but in that moment, we heard someone drive onto the property.

Ian strode for the door. "It's Damian. Stay here. Let me talk to him."

When the door closed, Pearlie and I jumped out of our chairs and peeked through the shades.

Ian hung onto the door of the truck in a vain attempt to get his nephew to see reason.

Damian shouted at his uncle, then put the truck in gear and leaped over a barrier into a flowerbed. Dragging limp geraniums and asters behind him, he raced for the main road and disappeared.

Ian, head down, trudged back to the house, and by the time he yanked open the door, we were back in our seats.

"He apologized for the window," he said, tossing Pearlie her cell phone as he headed for the kitchen.

Leaning on the open door of the fridge, he asked, "What time do you have?"

"Uh, two-thirty," I said, glancing at my watch.

"Good enough for me."

I heard the clink of bottles. "Either of you ladies want a beer?"

Pearlie grinned. "Whatcha got, Sheriff?"

"Pacifico or Tecate."

"Either is fine with me," Pearlie said.

"How about you, Lalla?" Ian asked.

"I guess I'm driving, so no thanks," I said, frowning at my cousin.

Pearlie tossed me her keys, happy to be in the position to accept a beer.

The fridge door was kicked shut and Ian handed Pearlie a Tecate.

"Where I come from," she said, "you could hyphenate Tecate with Texas and no one would think anything of it."

The sheriff raised his beer in salute. "Where in Texas are you from Ms. Bains?"

"Southeast Texas. My granny has a cattle ranch that reaches almost to Mexico. Sheriff, I know something about wanting to find out more about a father. My mom and dad were killed in an auto accident when I was in my teens. I didn't even know I had kinfolk until my dad's lawyer handed me the letters sent to my dad from his mother. She had disowned him on a count of his wild living, so I figured I'd hunt her down, spit in the eye of the mean old bat who would abandon her only son. I discovered how wrong I was, but it was only her patience that finally weeded the hurt out of my pasture."

Ian nodded thoughtfully. "If you'll give me a day, I'll see that he pays you for the broken window."

"Ah, now Sheriff," Pearlie said, "you're looking to rein in a troubled boy. But that broken window is not the problem here. Someone murdered Ron Barbour and set his house to blow, which means Damian could be in that killer's sights too."

Ian glanced down at his hands and asked, "Ron Barbour didn't tell you he was working on this case?"

Pearlie grimaced. "It kinda looked like Ron never intended to share this case with us."

Ian's head shot up. "Are you saying…?"

Pearlie answered with a snort.

"We knew he had some questionable parts to his otherwise sterling character," I said, "but stealing clients from our partnership has left us pretty much in the lurch."

"If he weren't already dead," Pearlie said, "I'd sure have motive to kill him."

Ian shook his head. "I can see you would have cause. I've sent Damian to my sister and told him to stay put, but I don't have to tell you that this man may also think you know who he is."

I felt a shock run under my skin. We'd been so distracted by our recent discovery of Ron's double-dealing, we'd overlooked our own vulnerability.

Ian got up to see us out to our car. "You two keep a low profile now, won't you?"

Pearlie winked to show Ian she wasn't worried and patted the zippered compartment on her purse. "We'll be careful. Besides, I've got my Pearlie special and Lalla has Caleb Stone. I think we'll be just fine."

In the rear-view mirror I saw him watch us leave, arms crossed; a man ready for whatever came his way. I wish I felt so confident.

"So what's the sheriff's story?" Pearlie asked.

"He's a good man. Caleb certainly respects him. Other than that, I know he was a homicide detective in Chicago before he and his wife moved back to Arizona and he joined the sheriff's office. Caleb said his wife died of cancer a few years back."

"We still have an appointment with Detective Hutton," Pearlie said. "I'm taking one of Ron's beaters, which I may or may not fill up before I bring it back."

I laughed. "You can pay for the gas or not, but I don't think it makes any difference to Ron, he's already dead."

Chapter Seven:

I left the police station after my interview with Detective Hutton, feeling secure in the knowledge that the detective had nothing on me. I wasn't so sure about Pearlie. The detective might be looking to put something on her, but first he'd have to buy her dinner.

On the way home, I stopped by my dad's place. He was gone, but his Mexican workers were there. When I got out of the car, they all stopped what they were doing and watched. I greeted the crew boss and asked if he knew when Mr. Bains would be back.

He tilted his ball cap back and smiled innocently. "*Lo siento, señora. No hablo inglés.*"

"Oh, sure you do, Rafael. My dad said you went to high school in Douglas."

Grinning, he dusted off his hands and got to his feet. "Busted. I promised your dad if another real estate lady showed up, I'd pretend I couldn't speak English. Say hi to my cousins, will you? Otherwise, they'll think you're *la migra.*"

I smiled and waved. Immigration can be so annoying, especially when you don't have a green card. They politely nodded and smiled. "Did my dad say when he was coming back?"

"He said he was going to pick up some lumber."
"Lumber? For what?"

Rafe shrugged. "It's not for this job, we're just cleaning up."

"Okay," I said. My dad had been talking about getting wood to shore up the old beams in the mine so maybe that's what it was for. "Did he say when the truck would pour the concrete for the patio?"

"Mañana?"

Remembering that the Spanish word for tomorrow was *mañana*, I smiled and left. When a Mexican says *mañana*, what they really mean is, *who knows?*

~~~~~~~~~~

Caleb wasn't home yet, and since the afternoon temperature was still hovering around eighty degrees Fahrenheit, I took a beer outside and flopped down onto a padded lounge chair in the shade and admired the water feature we just put up in our garden.

The first thing I did after moving here was put in pretty plants, only to come out in the morning and see that javelina had torn them all out, including the beautiful blue agave chosen especially for its lovely color. The javelina didn't care about any part of the agave but the tender roots. Deer ate the flowers off the rose bushes and gophers devoured the rest. After that, we put in plants resistant to javelina, deer, and gopher. Lavender, geraniums, jasmine, and lantanas did well, especially after we added a five foot adobe wall to enclose the garden. The jasmine soon outgrew its trellis and climbed aboard the pergola to lend a sensuous fragrance to our summer evenings. We added garden lights, an automatic drip system for the plants and the world's biggest grill for the times we entertained.

During the daylight hours, the garden is always full of birds and butterflies, hummingbirds, cooing doves, noisy Mexican jays, colorful blue buntings, golden orioles and scarlet red cardinals.

I took a sip of my beer and watched a roadrunner hop up onto the adobe wall, eyeball the water feature set up for the birds and determining the yard safe, settle onto one of the strategically placed boulders and proceed to groom its feathers.

To me, roadrunners always appeared awkward with their skinny bodies, long narrow beaks. That is until I saw a lovely yellow butterfly pass too close and in a blink of an eye disappear down the gullet of the bird.

Looking at my watch, I checked on the chicken cacciatore I'd started this morning and decided there would be enough if Pearlie and my dad wanted to stay for supper. Dad because he was avoiding his landlady and Pearlie because she hadn't met anyone she wanted to date in the last few months. Of all the people I would imagine going through a dry spell for company, it sure wouldn't be my cousin. Pearlie attracted men of all ages, shapes and sizes. She bussed the weathered cheeks of old men, teased the young ones until they blushed and accepted dates from men whose long-distance careers guaranteed nothing other than the occasional date.

Thinking I must have missed seeing my dad cut through our property on his way to the mine, I left a note for Caleb and added that he could eat if he was hungry. It was more than likely he'd shower, have a beer and wait for me to return with Dad.

Unlocking the doors to the barn, I moved the quad out and dodging cow patties along with gopher holes and prickly mesquite, left for his mine. Though the mine was officially part of my wedding gift from my great-aunt Mae, I figured if the mine kept my dad happy and busy, it was his to keep.

My dad's Jeep and trailer were parked next to the tunnel entrance. I ducked my head into the cool, damp interior of the mine, thumbed on my flashlight and helloed into the cool, dark interior.

"I'm back here," he called. "But be careful where you walk."

Detouring around a pile of lumber, I turned on my flashlight and followed the beam of light to where he sat on a rock. He had a pick in one hand and a large rock in the other. An overhead battery operated lantern hung from a hook on a beam, but it was enough for him to work by.

"I think I got me some good looking rough. Here," he said, shoving a piece of quartz into my hand, "shine your flashlight on this baby. Turn it around. That's it."

I did as he said and was rewarded with a dull chunk of yellow. "Wow."

"Yeah. I didn't think I'd actually see real gold so close to the surface. After the last sample I sent off to the assayer's office, I thought we were played out."

"I'm glad to see you kept at it. This looks promising," I said, admiring the gold in the quartz.

"That's the story your great-aunt Eula Mae told everyone when she boarded up this mine all those years ago. It's also the one I've been telling anyone who asks."

"That should keep out poachers."

"Coupled with warnings of possible cave-ins, I guess most folks have forgotten it's here."

"Was there any truth to the cave-ins?"

"Nothing that I can see. But just in case, I brought back some six-by-sixes. Now that I'm sure there's a vein to follow, I'm going to shore up the overhead beams and start digging again."

I looked up at the beams and the sweaty rock over our heads. Water, as everyone knows, is a great mover of rocks and dirt, but it could spell trouble as well.

"Don't you think you'd better hire someone to help with this, Dad? It's a bit much for one person."

"And have someone snooping in here when I'm not around? No thanks."

"You could put a door and a lock on the entrance."

"Locks can be sawed off and a strong axe can take down a door."

"How about a steel door?"

"'I'm not having some darn stranger out here asking questions about my gold mine. A secret like this wouldn't last one day in Wishbone."

"I suppose you're right, but what about the new patio? Aren't you supposed to be overseeing your workers?"

"Rafael and his cousins are all but finished and with no forecasted rain, the contractor will start pouring the concrete tomorrow. So you see, I have nothing else to do with my time."

"I thought you enjoyed the company of your landlady."

"She wants me to become a vegetarian."

"Sounds like a good idea. You *are* a heart patient, you know."

"I'm a second hand vegetarian. Cows eat grass, I eat the cows, and I'm going to continue to enjoy eating that way till I die, thank you very much."

Which reminded me to ask, "Mentioning eating, how was lunch with Coco Lucero?"

"Fine."

"Just fine?"

"Sure," he said. "Her enchiladas are as tasty as anything our Juanita ever made." Using the pick he took a manly swing at the rock wall, sending dirt cascading down onto his head. Embarrassed, he coughed and waved away the dust.

Obviously, Rafael's doe-eyed aunt had made an impression. "But does she have references," I asked. "You know, as a housekeeper?"

"I know what you mean, but Juanita worked for us for almost forty years and she didn't have any references."

Somehow the comparison didn't quite fit. Juanita had been with us for forty years because my mother said that if anything happened to her we should keep Juanita, no matter what. My mother was right. We would've starved without Juanita.

I came back to the present when I heard a popping sound. The ceiling above us trembled and there was the distinct sound of wood breaking.

"What was that?" I whispered.

"Probably just the ground settling."

There was another popping sound and the light from the hanging lantern swayed up the walls and back.

When a cold breeze drifted across my neck, my throat seized up. "Caleb should be home by now," I said, swallowing hard. "I have crock-pot chicken cacciatore for dinner. Want to join us?"

"Sounds good to me," Dad said, pulling the lantern off the overhead beam. "I'll start shoring up those beams tomorrow."

I aimed my flashlight for the exit, now anxious to be out in the hot sun again.

With my dad following, I felt silly that I was so easily scared out of the mine. Yes, it was dark, cold and damp, but we weren't that far from the entrance.

"I thought you would have had enough of mines," I said over my shoulder. "Especially after falling into that mine pit and finding a dead body."

"Not the same thing. There was no way out of that pit except up and my rope busted, so there I stayed," he said. "Me and a dead guy. I would've been dead too, if you and that nice Karen Paquette and her dog hadn't found me when you did."

I heard another pop and this time, the side posts behind us folded onto their knees.

My dad shoved me toward the light and cried out, "The roof's coming down! Run, Lalla!"

I didn't need another warning and aiming the sickly beam of my flashlight toward the end of the tunnel, did as I was told. Stumbling over rocks in my path, waving my hands in front of my face, I coughed and sputtered and came to a stop. "The light's gone. Where-where's the exit?"

I struggled to find the opening, but he held onto my arm. "Wait!"

"No, Dad. We're almost out."

"We can't. The cave-in has stopped. It's over."

I jerked out of his grasp. "Then let's get out of here!"

He took the flashlight out of my hand and waved it around the walls and ceiling.

"It's holding," he said.

"What do you mean? What's holding?"

He moved the light from the ceiling down another rock wall. "Look for yourself."

All I could see was a wall of rock. I turned around in a circle looking for the way out. "Did we make a wrong turn?"

"There're no side tunnels. Just the one. The ceiling has collapsed in front and behind us. We're stuck in the middle until someone comes and digs us out."

I stuttered with fear. "How-how far away are we from getting out of here?"

"I'm not sure, maybe thirty more feet?"

I sighed in relief. "That's not far. I left Caleb a note that I was coming here. He'll have us out in no time."

"That's thirty feet of rock and wet dirt to move, Lalla. It may take a while longer than that."

What he wasn't saying was that we were walled into a pocket with limited air space. Talk about being between a rock and a hard place! In the dull glow of my flashlight, the bony ridge of my father's forehead and cheeks glowed and his eyes were shadowed so deeply that the image appeared to morph into a bone white skull.

"Turn off the flashlight," the white skull said. "We may be here for a while."

Chapter Eight:

"What time is it?" I asked.

"I'm guessing about ten minutes past the last time you asked and no, I won't turn on the flashlight so I can look again; it'll just wear down the batteries."

"Do you think they know we're in here?"

"'Course they do. Caleb and probably half of Wishbone—hell, just my luck—maybe all of Wishbone. I'll bet there're even some old timers out there, showing them how to dig." He sighed. "Guess my secret was never meant to last."

"Miners? They'd have to be really old, wouldn't they?"

"The Lavender mine closed in the 1970's and some of the retirees are still docents for the mine tour. They dress you up in yellow slickers and hardhats and you get to ride in the mine cars. We should do it sometime."

"If we ever get out of this mine, I'll consider it."

"Ah, don't be so negative," my dad said, hugging me a little closer.

"This from the man who isn't happy unless he has something to complain about. The weather or the number of house guests we had for my wedding."

"And your favorite attitude should be gratitude, missy," There was no light to see his expression, but his voice was only slightly defensive.

"Do you ever think about what you would've done for a living if you hadn't become an aero-ag pilot?"

"I dunno. It's a rare thing for a man to get paid for doing what he loves and I loved flying. I made some pretty good money, too. I was near to busting my buttons when I finally had the cash to pay off the mortgage on the ranch."

"But did you ever feel as if you had lost out on some unfulfilled destiny having to raise kids as a widower?"

He was quiet for a moment. "I used to think the ranch, my planes, trucks, even my business reputation were what defined me as a man. I thought of it as my investment, something I had a stake in that I could leave to my children. Then I had that heart attack and my life took a turn."

"Like what?"

"Like that my real investment was my family, my children. Oh, I know I was impatient with your brother, annoyed that he would rather be a set designer in San Francisco than fly airplanes, but I got over that and before he died, didn't I? And I haven't done such a bad job of raising you, have I?"

I sniffed back my tears and said, "Are you saying all this stuff because you think we won't get out of here alive?"

"Don't be silly. Of course we'll get out of here."

"But just in case, you're coming clean *now*?"

"Okay, okay. I know I wasn't easy on you, but I do believe that a pint of example is worth a gallon of advice."

Never mind that he spent his days after heart surgery dealing out orders for the business from his barcalounger, or that he tended to favor his anemic clients over more profitable ones. Still, I wouldn't have traded those years for anything, so I guess we were even.

"You were a damn good pilot; maybe better'n your brother ever would've been, too."

"Oh crap," I said with a moan. "We *are* going to die in here."

"Will you stop that? Danged if I ever pay you a compliment again."

"I'm sorry." I sniffled and thinking it best to change the subject, I said, "Do you ever dream about flying?"

"Every once in a while. But for some reason I'm not in an airplane, I've got my arms spread wide and I'm soaring over the earth, looking down on the San Joaquin Valley."

"Yeah, I dream like that, too," I said. "Kinda fun isn't it?"

"With Ron Barbour dead, you and Pearlie can still set up your own P.I. business, right?"

"I was thinking I'd build a greenhouse and raise hydroponic tomatoes."

He was quiet for a minute. "You're joking, right?"

"It's looking like the P.I. business may not happen after all."

"Sure it will. Just have Pearlie make up a card for your greenhouse tomatoes."

"If only." But since we were likely to be stuck here in the dark for a few more hours, I figured I might as well tell him what we'd discovered about Ron Barbour.

After explaining it all to him, I said, "I suppose you're going to tell me, *a fool and his money are soon parted.*"

"I don't think you're a fool for investing in a business. From what I've read, good investigators are in demand these days. And if Ron Barbour taught you girls as much as you say he did, then it's not a waste of your money. So tell me, who do you think killed Ron and what're you girls going to do about it?"

"I think Ron must've uncovered a suspect," I said. "And that person is still very much alive and willing to kill again to keep his secret."

"A man whose past can't stand the light of day will be dangerous. Think about it. His secret had been safe and secure all these years. Could Ron have found and tried to blackmail this man? And gotten killed for it?"

"If that's true, the killer has to be someone whose financial worth is wrapped up in their very important position in this community."

"Now you sound like a real P.I."

But since I couldn't do anything about it right now, I yawned and tried for a more comfortable position on the cold, hard surface of the dirt floor. "It's getting colder. I wonder if we'll die of hypothermia or just run out of oxygen."

He laughed and hugged me tighter. "We'll make it. They're digging for us right now. You'll see. Any minute now they'll be breaking through."

"I'd be hungry if I weren't so cold."

"Quiet," he said.

"I know, I know, don't be negative."

"Not that. I heard something. Wait—there."

I heard it too. It was the sound of rocks being moved, dropped, a man's voice.

I got to my knees and felt the rock wall vibrate. "They're coming. They're getting close!"

Dad pulled himself up to the wall. I put his hands next to mine so he could feel it, too. Nothing. Had I imagined it all?

I moved my hands to another cool rock, waiting for the sound of a voice, a movement, anything.

"There!" my dad said. "Wish I had my hammer or pick to signal them."

"Then we'll just have to start yelling," I said, and opening my mouth to draw in a lung full of weak oxygen, I saw a man's leather gloved hand break through.

I threw a hand up against the bright beam of light shattering our small, dark prison, then joyfully sobbed.

An excited voice pierced the hole. "They're here!"

Another hand, this one black with dust, the fingers ungloved and bleeding, yanked out another rock and reached through to grab my hand.

"Move back as far as you can, sweetheart. We're going to break through."

"Caleb!" I cried, thrilled to hear his dear voice.

We did as we were told and scrambled back until we were as far away as we could get from the breaking wall of rock.

Chapter Nine:

Swaddled in blankets, Caleb and another man led us out of the tunnel and into bright light and applause. After the hours spent in the pitch black of the mine, my eyes were having a hard time adjusting to daylight.

I saw people we knew, Pearlie, Sheriff Ian Tom, Karen Paquette and what looked like our entire Cochise County Search and Rescue team pushing close to grin, hug and slap us on the back.

"What time is it?" I asked.

"Two a.m.," Caleb said. "We've been at it all night, taking turns digging, bringing out rock until we pushed through. Your search and rescue unit set up a relief station with first aid supplies and hot coffee. I don't know what I would've done without them."

"Two a.m.? Then why is it so bright?"

"Someone brought klieg lights on stands so we could continue to work through the night."

We stepped into the crowd of well-wishers, all of them smiling and wiping tears from their dirt smeared faces. I gapped and stuttered my thanks. "I can't believe it. All these people?"

"Yes," The exhaustion in his voice was tinged with pride. "Off duty police officers, firemen, deputies and some miners whose expertise with mine collapse sure came in handy. They set up a rotation so there would be no down time. Someone was always digging."

I picked up his bruised and bleeding hands, my heart filled with love. "Oh, Caleb, you didn't rest."

"They forced food and coffee on me a few times, but I couldn't stop," he said, kissing the top of my dusty head. "Not until I knew you and your dad were alive and safe."

I broke out of his warm embrace long enough to thank our rescuers. I thanked them all and told them that I would never forget their bravery and kindness to me and my family. "And, if ever any of you need a helping hand, you've only to ask. Thank you my friends."

"Now," I said to Caleb, the last of my energy melting away. "Take me home."

As Caleb was about to settle me into the quad, I stopped. "Where's Dad?"

"He's talking to one of mining families, but I'll go ask if he's ready to go."

He came back from the tight group of people surrounding my dad and said, "Someone by the name of Gabby will bring him home later. Right now, it looks like he's made some new friends."

"That's good," I said, yawning.

~~~~~~~~~~

Showered, powdered and in my nightie, the draw of bed in a dark room didn't hold the appeal it usually did. "Can we sleep on the roof tonight? I haven't had my fill of open sky for today."

Caleb didn't bother to mention that it might rain. He simply nodded and went to get the sleeping bags and a lantern.

Tucked under double zippered sleeping bags, we snuggled in and drowsily contemplated the stars playing peeka-boo with the clouds.

The front door opened and shut, then the French doors to the patio were opened and conversation drifted up to the roof.

"Dad's home," I said.

"And it sounds like he's got company," Caleb said, sniffing at the smells of frying bacon and eggs.

"If you're hungry, we could go downstairs and join them."

"I'm good," he said. "You?"

"No, I'm too tired to eat."

I heard running water in the bathroom.

"Someone is making themselves at home," Caleb said.

"Dad is probably too keyed up to go back home tonight anyway. He knows where the blankets are," I said, yawning.

A moment passed and Caleb turned his head to look at me. "You have to close your eyes if you expect to sleep."

"I'm trying. I close my eyes, but I just can't seem to fall asleep."

"It's the aftermath of a crisis. You've got all the wrong chemicals swirling around in your brain. But I have the cure for that," he said pulling me to him.

I came willingly into his arms, knowing that making love with my husband was indeed the cure for what ailed me. Later, I dreamed of a large crow with bright black eyes circled overhead cawing... *Geronimo*.

When I awoke, it was morning and in the distance a mated pair of crows circled and flew off. I reached across for Caleb only to find he had quietly slipped out of bed. I could smell coffee brewing, so I pulled his pillow under my head and watched the morning light spread across the valley below us. Taking inventory after last night's events I decided that in spite of the danger we'd faced with the mine collapse, we had been remarkably lucky.

I loved this time of day. The air was crisp and clean from yesterday's rain and the foliage along the San Pedro, while still deep in shadow, glowed darkly green. The cottonwoods sheltered the river as well as a myriad of hummingbirds and the tiny crimson red flycatchers.

I got up, but left the sleeping bags where they were in case I again found four walls too close for comfort. Then again, any excuse for another night under the stars wasn't a bad thing.

Dad's friend was gone and last night's dishes were on the drying rack. Caleb was in the shower and my dad was snoring on the couch, a blanket drawn up under his chin. I poured two cups of coffee and waved one under his nose.

He awoke with a snort, sat up and rubbed the sleep out of his eyes. "Huh? What time is it?"

"Seven thirty."

"It's late," he said, accepting the cup of coffee and throwing off the blanket, he grunted at his rumpled clothing. "Is the bathroom free?"

"It is now," Caleb said, toweling his wet hair. The sight of the faded and tight jeans hanging low on his narrow hips never failed to impress me. Alone, I might be tempted to take him back to bed, but since my dad was here this morning it would have to wait.

"Thanks," Dad said, handing me his cup as he passed for the bathroom.

"What's your hurry? It's not Sunday, you don't go to church, or are you attending AA meetings now?"

"Don't be smart, missy. Wishbone's chapter of The Benevolent Society of Miners meets this morning," he said, shutting the bathroom door behind him.

In another minute, he came out of the bathroom, hair slicked back, white stubble on his chin.

"Don't you want...?" The door slammed before I could finish my question. "I guess he doesn't want breakfast," I said. "Or maybe the club holds their meetings at a donut shop."

"What?" Caleb looked up from pouring his coffee.

"Never mind. I'm starved. What's for breakfast?"

Chapter Ten:

Last night, intent on getting uninterrupted sleep from well-meaning neighbors and nosy news people, Caleb had disconnected the landline and turned off my cell. Booting my cell up again, I saw multiple messages from Tucson television stations and one from Pearlie with the succinct message to call her immediately, if not sooner, as she had a break in the case.

When Caleb passed me for the door, he stopped, turned around and came back to kiss me. I loved that he thought I needed an extra kiss, right up to the moment he whispered, "Try not to get in trouble today, will you?"

When I was sure he was gone, I returned Pearlie's phone call, figuring by now she'd be burning a new hole in the ozone with her news.

Instead, I got her voice mail. I left her a message and hung up, washed dishes, mopped floors, started a load of laundry and with a cup of tea sat down to watch the dryer gaily tumble our clothes dry. When my dad's jeep pulled into the driveway, I went outside to greet him.

"That was quick. Did your benevolent miners deny you membership already?"

My teasing stopped when I saw his face. "What's wrong?"

He took me by the elbow and led me into the house. "Let's get a cup of coffee and sit."

He poured us a cup and said, "I was flattered to be invited. After talking to these guys, I could see that I don't know as much about mining as I thought I did."

I did a hand roll for him to get on with his story.

"Gabby found something at the entrance of the mine. The fellas wanted to discuss it with me." He pulled some items from his pocket: a snippet of narrow gauge orange plastic tubing and a small amount of twisted electrical cord. He moved the twisted electrical cord in front of the other items. "This is what they would've used up to until about thirty or forty years ago as a fuse to a charge of dynamite."

He then replaced the wire with the orange tubing. "This is what is used today. It's called a non-el, for non-electric and it's what Gabby found on the ground just inside the entrance. The club members confirmed how easy it would be to set a charge of dynamite behind each of the posts. As soon as one set of posts fell, the cap, the ceiling and everything would tumble down after it. That popping sound we heard? That was charges going off. Lucky for us, a pocket was created when two posts didn't explode. It saved our lives."

"How? Why? Wait. I thought your mine was a secret."

"Well," he drawled, "I learned this morning that there are no secret mines in Arizona. First of all, the club has a map of all private mines. They're numbered by the state and county. The only secret about my mine was that I had reopened it. I'd say the cat was out of the bag the minute I bought those six by six posts yesterday. By lunchtime everyone in Wishbone knew I'd opened Aunt Mae's old mine and had plans to start working it."

"Then someone deliberately sabotaged the mine? Who would do such a thing?"

"As for who, that is something you get to work on, but Gabby thinks that at the very least, it was meant to slow down your investigation."

I could feel my hands clench into fists. "Slow *down* the investigation? Whoever thought that sure doesn't know me. Wait till I tell Caleb," I said pulling out my cell phone.

Dad grabbed my wrist. "Wait. Before you call Caleb, Gabby and a couple other fellas are coming over. They're righteously indignant that some ornery, low-down critter would sabotage a mine to murder innocent folk and they want to help."

I was thinking of Ron Barbour's untimely exit from life in a house explosion. Not so different from the mine collapse; both were made to look like an accident. This had to be the work of the same person. Someone was hoping to plug holes, which meant we were too close for comfort. I could only hope that we would get a lead before this killer got any closer.

"Do your friends have any ideas on who we should look at?" I asked.

"Well, the miners have a theory, but I'll let Gabby explain."

Just as I picked up the phone to call him, Caleb arrived, herding three strangers ahead of him.

Dad stood to greet the visitors. "Lalla, this is Ben Tucker and Ronny Barns. Gabby here runs some cattle, but she's also a miner," my dad said, with a blush.

Gabby cheerfully stuck out her hand and in a voice like gravel being dragged along by a back-hoe, said, "Gabby Hayes. Pleased to meet you."

Her hand was calloused like a man's and the lines radiating from the corner of her mouth put her at about sixty years' worth of Arizona sun. The gravelly voice probably due to years of smoking. Good thing I quit when I did, or in another twenty years, I'd sound just like her.

Silver hair clips and dangling turquoise earrings added a feminine touch. There was no doubt that Gabby was all woman. If I had some weight on my bones and worked out of doors for most of my life, we could be mistaken for cousins.

"I suppose you're wondering about the odd name," she said.

Behind her back, Caleb winked and I tried not to smile.

"The name's Gabriella, but folks 'round here have called me Gabby since I was three. Didn't give it much thought until *after* I married Mike Hayes and folks started ribbing me some about it. That lasted until the next inter-estin' thing came along. So me 'n' the husband got gold fe-ver after we discovered an old mine on my dad's place. It's a lot like Noah's, but thank God nobody's tried to kill us in it."

I pointed everyone to the dining table. When we were all seated, Gabby acted as spokesperson for the miners. "Let me start with what we do know. A mine collapse is big news in Wishbone and I don't think we've had one in forty years. We think if you look at the videos and photos from both the mine collapse and that fire at Ron Barbour's place, you might find your man."

I gasped. "One of those nice people who stayed until 2 a.m. tried to kill us?" My feelings of good will for all our rescuers just took a dive. "Surely we can rule out the police, sheriff's deputies and fire department."

Caleb winced. "I wish that were true, but at this stage, I don't think we should rule out anyone. There were two vans from Tucson and a photographer from the Sierra Vista

Herald. Leave this to me, I'll get the video and photos from both scenes."

I could feel my temperature rise at the idea of being excluded. "Pearlie and I can do that."

"The mine collapse is now an attempted homicide," he said. "It's my jurisdiction."

"It's my case, too, Caleb."

Caleb, seeing I was about to explode, defused my temper with a question. "Where's Pearlie?"

"I don't know," I said, still smarting at his attempt to take over. "She's not returning my calls."

My breath caught in my throat and I blanched. Had she stepped in front of the same killer who'd murdered Ron Barbour and tried to kill my dad and me?

Before I started to hyperventilate, my cell rang. I was relieved to see it was Pearlie calling.

"Guess who who's back at the gym!"

"Damian, I suppose?" Ian Tom did say the kid wasn't one to follow orders. "Where are you now, Pearlie?"

"I got hungry, okay?"

"Fine, fine," I said. Pearlie tended to get defensive about her eating habits. Food was a way to keep her anxieties at bay. I got anxious and stopped eating. I really should be grateful; she could've taken to drink like our former business partner.

~~~~~~~~~~

By the time Pearlie arrived, Gabby and her friends had left so Caleb, my dad and I took turns explaining the suspicious circumstances of the mine collapse.

"So, you two can investigate," he said, closing his notebook, "up to a point."

Pearlie flicked two fingers in concession. "Sure, but videos and photos are as available to us as they are to law enforcement, you know."

"Thanks for reminding me." He rubbed a hand across his forehead. "Lalla, Ian Tom wants to meet us at his house."

"Today?"

He looked at his watch. "As soon as we can get there."

"I'll ride with Pearlie."

Caleb's lips tightened as he fought to come up with an appropriate response to my assertion that Pearlie was invited as well, but gave up and marched for the door.

"What's with him?" Pearlie asked.

"Sometimes he acts too much like a cop," I said, and seeing she was still driving the cat-piss smelling rental, asked, "when do you get your Jeep back?"

She muttered something that might've been a cuss word, so I changed the subject. "How was your lunch?"

"Lunch? Oh, the usual, I guess."

"You said you stopped to eat... or did I misunderstand?"

"One of the trainers at the gym and I got to talkin' and I guess we sorta have a date tonight."

"That's nice. Is he someone who can help us keep tabs on Damian?"

"I don't know and I don't care. He's cute and I'm not going to look at his resume and you better not, either."

"Okay." Pearlie had reason to be touchy. Her choices for male companionship had a way of getting dissected by her granny and though Great Aunt Eula Mae was only trying to help keep her granddaughter from making another bad choice, it didn't do much for Pearlie's love life. I wasn't a snitch and had no intention of tattling on my cousin. She was quite capable of getting out of her own mistakes.

~~~~~~~~~~~~~~

The last time Pearlie and I were in Ian Tom's house it was quiet and calm. This time we walked into a rowdy argument between Ian and his nephew.

Ian formally introduced Caleb, Pearlie and me to his nephew, Damian White, whose only acknowledgement was to crack his knuckles and stare at the floor.

"Damian," Ian snapped.

The kid stuck his fingers between the seat cushions of the sofa to keep them still.

Ian glared at his nephew. "I've agreed to allow him to continue his training as long as he keeps decent hours and leaves the investigation into his father's death to the professionals, right, son?"

Damian complied with an indifferent shrug.

Hoping to pry apart his hostile attitude, I started with a question. "What do you do for work, Damian?"

I looked to Ian for an interpretation of the kid's mumbling response.

Ian's jaw tightened. "I guess he's got hoof and mouth disease. Iron work, right, Damian? On high rises in Las Vegas. Go on, tell them."

Damian's head came up off his chest. His eyes flashing angrily. "You know."

"Some of it, but you can tell it better than I can. It's an interesting story."

Damian glared at each of us, but something akin to pride took over the defiant attitude. "One of my buddies got me tickets to the Las Vegas finals of American Ninja

Warrior. The minute I saw that show, I knew I had what it took to win, but I didn't have the training and the show looks for contestants with a story, you know? When I told them I was Apache and a Native American ironworker, they flipped. A combination like that could take me all the way to the top."

"Native American ironworkers?" I asked.

"Mohawks from Canada started coming to New York as early as the 1900's. White men liked to say that it was because *injuns* weren't afraid of heights, but that's not so. They were just braver. They could walk any beam at any height. Then they got work riveting. That was real money for people who were used to scraps to live on. They were there when the planes crashed into the twin towers. One said it flew so low, he could see the rivets in the fuselage."

Now that his defensive posture had loosened, I asked, "Tell us about your father, Damian."

His eyes darted from his uncle to me. "Whadya wanna know?"

"What makes you think he was murdered?"

"My dad told my mom they were out to get him and one deputy in particular called him a nigger. My father was also half Apache, but in those days the whole county was racist."

Ian Tom sighed. "You read the report, Damian. You know it didn't start out that way. The folks in Palominas have always been a mixed race community."

Damian's eyes flashed. "That doesn't change anything. Someone still shot my dad in the back."

Sheriff Tom slapped his hands on his knees. "And that's where you folks came in. But since I have no intention of driving a wedge between you and your bride, Caleb, I need to ask your permission."

Caleb's mouth twitched in that way it did when he wasn't going to like the question. "What kind of permission do you have in mind, Ian?"

"Damian's mother, my sister, Naomi, would like to hire Lalla and Pearlie to finish the job Ron started."

Pearlie, unable to contain herself, issued a happy squeak.

Caleb grimaced. "You know, Ian, every once in a while I dream that I have some kind of say-so about what my wife does or doesn't do—and then I wake up."

Ian, looking unsure if he was being kidded or not, said, "Is that a yes?"

I laughed. "And to think, he married me anyway."

"Then we have a deal?" Ian asked.

I looked at Pearlie. She grinned and stuck out her hand. "Deal."

"A couple of things: First, my nephew has agreed to cooperate and second, my sister is somewhat fragile, so if you have any question about this case, please bring them to me."

Pearlie nodded eagerly, but I wasn't satisfied with Ian's request about his sister. "What do you mean by fragile? Is your sister ill?"

"No, not anything like that. It's just that she lives quietly. She's an artist you know and I'd rather you gave whatever news you have with your investigation to me. Can you do that?"

I looked at Pearlie. Her eyes were telegraphing a plea to just say yes.

I agreed with a quick lift of my shoulders.

"Good," he said. "I told you I looked at all the deputies involved in the shootout, but that was before my sister hired a P.I. I'm giving you a copy of the entire file, pictures included. I found a few things, but… "

"But what, Sheriff?" Pearlie asked.

"You will have to tread carefully. I have taken the liberty of writing up a list of possible suspects. It's down to three men. They all have at least one reason to want to avoid any association with your investigation into this old murder."

Ian reached for the folder on his coffee table and handed it to me. "The check is from my sister but I am concerned enough about this list to put a letter into a safety deposit box with a key for my attorney. If anything happens to me or my nephew, the state's attorney will get a copy. Please put this in a safe place, or better yet, memorize the names and burn it."

Pearlie flipped open the folder, read it and then passed it over to me. I read the names and with a lighter from the table the document faded into black ash. "How about the autopsy on Ron Barbour?"

Pearlie shivered. "If it's all the same to you, I'll pass."

"A copy of the report is all we need," I said, patting her hand. I wouldn't expect my squeamish cousin to want to watch as Ron's body was laid open on a steel table, his internal organs incised and weighed by an indifferent medical examiner.

"I can get you a copy when it's official."

I picked up the photo of the horse with Geronimo engraved on the frame. "Is there some significance in the name Geronimo to you and your family?"

Ian looked at his nephew before answering. "Outside of raising champion quarter horses, we're his direct descendants."

"That's also your nickname at the gym, isn't it, Damian?" Pearlie asked.

"What of it?" Damian was back to his belligerent attitude.

Ian's jaw tightened and his face went red with frustration. "You broke into this nice lady's office and stole her personal property. For some reason she has decided not to turn you over to the police, but keep it up and she might change her mind."

Damian ducked his head as if he wished he could disappear.

"You can help us with this investigation, you know," I said.

"Perhaps you'd rather remain a suspect in Ron Barbour's murder?" Ian said. "Then what do you think your chances are for a shot at American Ninja Warrior?"

Startled, Damian's coppery skin actually paled. "Sorry."

"Ian," I said, looking at the check. "We can't accept this. Your sister already gave Ron a deposit."

He pushed it back to me. "You'll have to finish what Ron started and without the evidence he had to get an arrest. Hopefully, you can get what you need without getting killed for it."

Since he put it that way, maybe we should have asked for more money.

Chapter Eleven:

Outside Ian Tom's house, Caleb leaned on the open window of Pearlie's rental and sniffed. "Is it just me or does your rental smell like cat piss?"

"I have no idea what you're talking about," Pearlie said, avoiding his eyes. "And if you'll excuse us, we have a job to do."

He looked at me. "You'll take Ian's advice and keep a low profile, right?"

"We can't get in trouble looking at pictures of the house fire and the mine collapse, now can we?" I said sweetly.

"I've seen you get into trouble with less."

"This ain't our first rodeo, you know," Pearlie said.

"Then I'll let you get to it," Caleb said, stepping away.

Pearlie put the car into gear and hit the gas.

Either she was anxious to get some miles on our first real paying job or she was thinking about her date later tonight with the trainer from the gym.

~~~~~~~~~~~

Arriving at our office in Sierra Vista, Pearlie breezed through the door without using her key.

"You didn't lock it?"

"Why bother?" Pearlie said. "Except for Clyde here, anything worthwhile went up in flames with Ron."

Today our skeleton wore a ratty old wig, a ball cap and reading glasses taped to its non-existent nose.

"What's with the book in his hands?"

"I thought one of us should look busy."

"We did all the work on most of his cases for the last three years," I said, peeling off my jacket and opening my laptop.

"Evidently not *all* of them," Pearlie said.

"Well, we're busy now, so quit accessorizing the skeleton."

"We should hire a secretary," Pearlie said.

"We don't have the money," I growled.

"We have two jobs on the books. We finish them and we'll have some cash to pay part-time help."

"Today is Tuesday. How are we supposed to finish our two insurance jobs and find Ron's killer in just one week? And lock the damn door, will you?"

Pearlie ignored my grumpy behavior and turned the lock on the office door. "Not that this will keep Damian out. Alrighty then. I'll start with online newspaper stories and then check out the Tucson TV station's for video or print, add up all the people we can ID and if they show up at both places, I'll make copies for comparison. You work on Ian's names."

"Right," I said scooting up to the desk. Though it went against everything I had learned about the men on the list, if Ian had cause to mention them, we'd work on it. I'd dig into property owned or mortgaged, marriages, divorces, bankruptcies, anything that showed vulnerability or a willingness to murder in order to keep a secret.

"Will Caleb match our unknowns with the national database?" Pearlie asked.

"Yes, but I'm hoping it's some local low-life we helped put in jail over the last couple of years."

"Maybe it's one of Ron's. He worked on a lot of criminal cases."

Five hours later, Pearlie leaned back in her chair and stretched. "Whoever said being a P.I. was glamorous should be shot—twice."

I moved my shoulders around to ease the cramp in my neck. "Once for thinking it and once for saying it out loud?"

"Yep."

Pearlie came up with five matches for both places. "Some are in uniform and a couple could simply be off-duty volunteers, but you'll have Caleb double check for us? Criminal records, outstanding warrants, right?"

"Yes," I said. I was not looking forward to giving the list to Caleb. I was on a first name basis with two of them and the other one was a close friend of Caleb's.

I started with what I'd found out about Wishbone's favorite TV car salesman, Wade Hamilton. "I got the police report on it. Five years ago Wade Hamilton hired Ron to investigate the theft of cars from his lot and he paid the bill with our surveillance cars."

"Those two junkers?" Pearlie snickered. "I'd say Wade got the better end of that deal. So what was the case about?"

"The police report says Wade had a twenty year old kid, by the name of Joey Green, washing the cars. Ron testified in the trial that the kid used Wade's cars to rob businesses then sold them to chop shops on the border."

"Where's the kid now?" Pearlie asked.

"He's out on parole, working at a wrecking yard in Benson. I think one of us should pay him a visit."

Pearlie propped her head onto her hands and said, "Wade Hamilton. Wade Hamilton."

I waited until the count of ten before nudging her. "What?"

She popped out of her chair. "We actually have a file on it. It's in the closed cases."

Pearlie started noisily shuffled through the file cabinet.

"Got it," she said, waving the file over her head. "It had a red tag for *closed case*, so I didn't bother with it."

"See? We should go through these old cases, maybe dig up more business."

"When we have time." She opened the file and read. "Wade Hamilton hired Ron Barbour to uncover who was stealing the cars. It looks like Ron did a week's worth of surveillance for this job. He got expenses and those two nifty Fords we use for surveillance. Wait. There's something..." she sifted through paperwork and stapled receipts, then looked up and grinned. "If I didn't know what a liar and a cheat Ron was I would never have bothered to look at these receipts."

"Well?"

"All of his expenses for the case are stamped with dates *after* the kid was arrested and there's no receipt for a check on the job. He probably took cash so he wouldn't have to report it on his taxes."

I thought for a minute. "I think it might be worse than that, Pearlie. Think about it. Cash and two old cars for all that work?"

"You're thinking he didn't actually do any work?" she asked.

"I think Ron was only too happy to write up a report after the robberies."

Pearlie's disgust only matched my own. "And perjured himself with his testimony? In court! I'd be shocked, but on top of everything else, I guess I'm not. I have to wonder what deal Joey got to keep quiet."

"Better yet, did Ron try to blackmail Wade to keep his secret?" I asked.

"Oh. That would explain Wade offing Ron, but coming so close on the heels of this investigation, was Ron about to name Wade as Damian's father's killer?"

"*If* Ron had evidence that confirmed Wade as the shooter," I said.

"Then Ron's attempt to blackmail Wade backfired. Well, it's something to keep in mind, but it's not hard evidence. Who else do you have on the list?" Pearlie asked.

"This is a hard one; Jesse Jefferson."

Pearlie leaned forward in her chair. "Are you sure? He's Wishbone's favorite preacher. How was he involved with Miracle Faith Church?"

"He was an early convert, but by the time of the shooting he was already working to help members who wanted out. There's no record of him being at the shooting, but Ian said he has a secret."

"Like what?"

"Money problems," I said.

"Oh please. All preachers have money problems. I dunno, Lalla. All of these men are prominent in Wishbone. What if Ian Tom is using us to compromise their integrity so he can be assured of another term as sheriff?"

"You're awfully cynical these days, Pearlie Mae."

"You can blame Ron for that," she said. "I don't remember seeing a file with Jesse Jefferson's name on it. What if he didn't have any connection to Ron?"

"Maybe no connection to Ron, but you're the best person to look into Jesse's finances and I'll try to find out if he had critics."

Pearlie finished her notes and looked up. "You have one more name, right?" When I wouldn't meet her eyes, she said, "It's not your husband, is it?"

"No, but it's close enough to home to make me think I'm going to regret ever taking this job."

"Like we have a choice?"

Chapter Twelve:

"You have a date tonight," I said. "Caleb can pick me up here."

"Don't worry about it," Pearlie said, picking up her purse. "I'm meeting him in Wishbone anyway, so it's on my way."

"Don't you want to go home and shower first?"

"Oh," she said, lifting her arm and sniffing. "I guess I better. Come and help me find something to wear. Half-an-hour tops, okay?"

I should have known better. Her hair alone took a half-an-hour and she spent another half hour pawing through her closet for just the right dress. "Gotta wear something nice, but not too fancy... no, no and definitely not *that* one. That's what I wear to funerals."

"I thought it looked familiar," I said, hanging it back in the closet. Funerals were a good place to finger skip-traces.

Two hours later, Pearlie let me out at the door of my house.

When I saw my dad's Jeep, I groaned. I needed an hour with Caleb alone. One of the men on the list was someone my husband liked, respected and spent time with. And of all the dirty secrets that Ian alluded to, this was the most ruinous. Never mind this man's reputation in the community, even a whiff of an accusation could send him to prison and I dreaded the scene it would cause with Caleb.

Still, the smell of food wafting through the front door put me into a much better mood.

Wearing my apron, Dad pulled a tin-foil wrapped casserole out of the oven. "You're just in time to set the table."

I sniffed. "Gee, now this smells a lot like Juanita's enchilada casserole."

"It does, doesn't it? Picked it up at that Mexican café outside of Wishbone. Oh, and set another place, will you? My friend Gabby is coming to supper."

Looking for a hint of what this was all about, I asked, "What's the occasion?"

"The foundation for my patio was poured today and when it's dry, I want my dog back. You can have him any time you need him to track dead people."

"Dad, that's for cadaver dogs. Hoover's an air scent dog; he looks for lost people."

"Good for you, Hoover," Dad said, congratulating the dog. "Gabby has some information about your murder case… oh, there she is," he said, removing the apron and heading out of the door.

From his bed by the door, Hoover's big ears pricked up and he rose to his feet, switching his gaze from me to the door.

"Stay," I said, and he dropped down again, his eyes on the door.

I set another place at the dinner table and seeing my husband walk by, gave him a light kiss.

"It was nice of your dad to bring supper," he said, taking the plates from my hands. "But please tell me he's not moving back in."

"I don't think that's what he meant by bringing us dinner, but he did invite Gabby to eat with us."

"I saw them talking outside. I better go wash up then. Smells like Juanita's cooking." He added another kiss as he slid past me for the bathroom.

The memory of our housekeeper's wonderful seven layer enchilada casserole brought back wonderful memories. I was pretty dense in those days, wallowing in self-pity from my second divorce and not paying attention to my childhood friend's own marriage problems. Everyone else knew Caleb and his wife had separated. Our good friend and café owner, Roxanne, made sure he had a breakfast sandwich to go every morning on his way to work as sheriff of Stanislaus County and my dad, who could be completely clueless about my problems, made sure Caleb had a standing invitation at our house for a weekly meal.

We'd been friends since we were each orphaned of a parent; his father, my mom, leaving behind two lonely and frightened children. It was only natural that we gravitated to each other for support. We thought it fun that our tall, pale blond Nordic looks made people incorrectly assume we were related, but after my two to his one failed marriage, I finally came to understood what I'd been missing all those years. Now, after three years of marriage, I can honestly say that I've never been happier.

I wondered if the ingredients for the enchilada casserole my dad brought home from the Mexican café really was that much like Juanita's, or was I confusing it with Coco Lucero's enchiladas?

The front door opened and booted steps clicked over the Saltillo tiles.

Gabby was in a clean, if faded, western shirt, jeans and a silver concho belt inlaid with turquoise the size of my fist.

"I brought some homemade wine," she said, laying a gallon jug on the counter. "Careful there. I cleaned it some but it's a mite damp and can slip outta yer hands." She rubbed her work-worn hands together and smacked her lips. "Somethin' sure smells good. Where do I sit?"

I set the jug of wine on the dining table. "Any place you like. Actually, everyone have a seat and I'll bring out the food. Not you, Caleb," I said, keeping him with me.

"Is Gabby your dad's new lady friend?" he asked.

"I haven't a clue, but I suppose we'll find out soon enough," I said.

Caleb playfully pinched my butt and then balancing the bowl of salad on one hand and the dressing in the other, carried it out to the dinner table.

Gabby poured everyone a glass of her homemade wine. "Don't let this nice red fool you. It's high octane an' been known to kick more than one cowboy on his ass."

While the food was passed around, Gabby proceeded to regale us with her family's history. "My pa was an out of work miner and hired on as ranch hand at my grampa's place. Within a year he was managing the ranch and married to the owner's daughter. They spent their honeymoon prospecting, then came home to discover an old mine on grampa's property. My husband and I worked it off and on until he died a few years back."

She accepted our murmurs of sympathy and nodded at the wine. "Pass that over here one more time, will ya? The Hayes family has been making their own wine for nearly a hundred years." Upending her third glass of the evening, she poured another. My first and only glass was mostly empty, but I wasn't about to finish it. This stuff was pure TNT.

Maybe Gabby could absorb the alcohol without it affecting her, but Caleb's eyes were glassy after one. Thinking one of us should be sober enough to say goodnight to our guests I pushed the pitcher of iced water over to him. He poured a full glass and thanked me with a quick wink.

"Tell Lalla and Caleb about the other thing," Dad prompted.

Gabby reddened at the sudden attention. She cleared her throat and in her buzz-saw voice said, "Well, Noah here says you and your cousin worked for Ron Barbour?"

I sighed and blew out of breath of frustration. "I guess you could call it that." When Gabby's pale eyebrows went up, I smiled sweetly to show that I was only kidding.

"Well, I don't know if this will help or not, but I was a new school teacher in Palominas back when that religious cult moved here. Damian White was a little tyke then and as happy with math and science as he was with recess. But after meeting his folks at a parent teacher conference, I knew that there was trouble in that family. The missus was Native American, you know and besides the fading bruise on her cheek, I noticed the boy always stayed on his ma's side and away from his pa. Then that preacher lady insisted all the church children get homeschooled and Damian's ma came by to see where she could buy school books and such. When I asked if she needed help in getting loose from her husband, she shook her head and said she already had plans for him. That was the last time I ever spoke to her, but I read about the shoot-out in the papers."

Under the table, Caleb gave my knee a cautionary squeeze.

I returned the squeeze to show he didn't have to worry about what I might say. "What did you think of her comment about having plans for her husband?"

"Well," she said, touching her earring. "I don't rightly know that I gave it much thought until I read about it in the papers, him gettin' killed an' all. I hope you don't think I'm gossiping or nothin'. Noah and I thought you might like to know."

"Thank you, Gabby. I do appreciate it. It's an old cold case and there are never enough leads."

Gabby returned the smile. "You're surely welcome. Now did someone say there was pie for dessert?"

She accepted only the smallest piece of apple pie and then bid us all good night.

Caleb stood at the kitchen window, his hands in sudsy water and said, "They have matching Jeeps."

"Then that's another thing they have in common."

"She also finished off that gallon of wine she brought."

"You think she shouldn't be driving?" I asked.

"Your dad's getting in his Jeep. He'll follow her home."

"That's nice of him," I said.

Caleb wasn't much of a drinker. A beer or two once a week was more his speed, so I remarked on the two glasses he drank.

"I've never tasted anything quite like it," he said. "Not too much tannin and that little bit of sparkle was a nice touch. I wonder how she makes it?"

My eyebrows went up in surprise. "Since when have you become a wine connoisseur?"

He grinned and kissed me. "Just another level to the marvelous man you married. But thanks for cutting me off when you did or I'd be wearing a bad hangover tomorrow morning. So what do you think about Gabby's take on Naomi White?"

"If she shot her husband, why pay us to find his killer?"

Caleb shrugged. "Just because she's paying you doesn't mean she actually expects you to succeed."

I couldn't help feeling the old fear of defeat edging in on me. "Not you too? Everyone in this county seems to think we couldn't possibly know anything about investigating, much less be able to solve this case."

He reached over and hugged my shoulders. "I do, your dad does, and Modesto's police chief sure remembers what you did for him. He'll vouch for you any time you need it."

"I guess I just hate to think that Ian purposely did not mention his sister."

"Ian Tom has only been back in Arizona for eight years and he may not know everything about his sister's history with her husband. But if the evidence points to her, we'll deal with it."

"I haven't told you the names on that list yet, have I?"

"I figured you would when you were ready," he said, wiping his hands on a dishtowel.

"Wade Hamilton, Jesse Jefferson and I know it sounds crazy," I said, waiting for the outburst, "Andy Sokolov is the third person."

Caleb's back stiffened. "Say again?"

I was getting a headache, maybe a migraine, and I hadn't had one in years. I rubbed my forehead, trying to ease into the subject of Caleb's best friend and mayor of Wishbone.

"If it's any consolation, Pearlie thinks the sheriff may be aiming his sights on a political career, so nabbing a killer who is a respectable member of Wishbone's society would be quite the coup, wouldn't it?"

"I have to trust that there's a reason why Ian gave you these names. Besides shooting a man in the back and then covering it up, Ian's offered you some leads to follow. Have you come up with anything yet?"

"We've just started to look, but five years ago Wade Hamilton hired Ron Barbour to uncover who was stealing cars off his lot. The car thief was a kid he had washing cars."

"But what?"

"As far as Pearlie is concerned, his worst offense was accepting those two old junkers we use for surveillance, but the most damning evidence of Ron's corruption were his expense receipts. His receipts don't match his report."

"You're saying he lied in the report to keep his pal in the clear?"

"And perjured himself on the witness stand. We're also thinking Ron made the deal and kept Wade's secret, but then later tried to squeeze him for more money."

"And got himself killed for his efforts? The kid went to prison. Is he out now?"

"He's out on parole," I said, "employed at a wrecking yard in Benson and keeping his nose clean."

"Do you want me to talk to him?"

"Pearlie or I will do that."

"Who's next?"

"Jesse Jefferson."

"Jesse? Dammit, Lalla, I have Rotary breakfast with him once a month. We've been to his church. He's one of the nicest people I know."

"Ian didn't say he wasn't. He only said to look for money problems."

"Oh, all right," he said with a wave of his hand. "Then let's get the elephant out of the closet and in the room, shall we? What's Andy's secret?"

I looked at my feet, dreading the outcome of this conversation. Either way, it wasn't going to end well.

"Ian could be wrong," I said.

"For Chris' sake, Lalla, what's Andy supposed to have done? Kiddy porn?"

I blanched.

"Oh Jesus!" he said, collapsing onto a kitchen chair.

"There were only two words after Andy's name, child pornography."

Caleb simply shook his head, staring at me as if I were an alien creature. "If I didn't have so much respect for Ian Tom, I'd suspect Pearlie was right thinking about a political agenda. Dammit. If it turns out his lead was from some jealous rumor monger I'll personally kick his ass."

Hoping to divert his attention away from this dreadful subject, I asked, "Did you feed Hoover already?"

"I did," he said, tightly. "I would *never* betray a pal."

Sick at heart, I went to bed while Caleb stayed up, the living room light and TV on, better to think about what I'd just told him.

The other side of our bed remained cold and empty until my restless sleep was interrupted by a phone call from county search and rescue. "We have a lost Alzheimer's patient," the caller from the sheriff's office said. "Karen Paquette is out of town and we need an air scent dog. Bring Hoover."

Chapter Thirteen:

Our search and rescue team had been out for most of the night in search of an elderly native American Alzheimer's patient.

I looked up to see the Milky Way lighting a brilliant path across the sky, the result of yesterday's rain scrubbing the ever present dust out of the atmosphere.

I tugged at the neck of my padded jacket in an attempt to keep the cold out. That nagging feeling was back, the one that said this search and rescue for an Apache wasn't going to go well. But then it had been a long night and the last of my reserves were just about shot.

He had wandered away from his daughter's home, about five miles from the tiny hamlet named after the rugged and remote Dragoon Mountains.

We were told only the basics, that he wasn't one to miss a meal and never left the house after dark and that she'd searched on her own, then enlisted neighbors and finally admitting defeat, called 9-1-1.

When Hoover found the man's trail, I had to lean back to keep his stride in check.

"Slow down boy," I said, the leash in my hand a taut line between us.

If I couldn't keep him under control, the dog could easily bound away and out of sight. Soon he had us trotting in a southerly direction, down through an empty arroyo and up again, trailing six footsore men in our wake.

"Crap," I said. "He's headed for the Cochise Stronghold." This was where Cochise and his legendary band of Chiricahua Apache played hide and seek with the American Cavalry and if Hoover's nose was right, it was also where an old Apache was making his last stand.

With sunlight firing the tips of the pinnacles above us, Steve pointed out a well traveled animal path. "It'll be easier going now," he said.

We stopped to reconnoiter with the team to the west of us. Sloshing the contents of his thermos around, Steve shoved it into my hands. "Drink up."

I tried to wave him off, but he wouldn't take no for an answer. "Don't be a ninny. This is high desert and even on the coldest day you can still get dehydrated."

What he wasn't saying was that I needed to follow orders. I smiled my thanks and gulped down the last of his lukewarm tea.

While Hoover worked the trail, Steve gave us a history lesson. "Outstanding runners, the Apache. Deep chested, and except for Cochise who was reported to be six feet tall, no more'n a few inches over five feet. The Apache toughened their boys by having them throw rocks at each other."

"That sounds harsh," someone said.

"It was duck or die," Steve said. "Rocks and then bows and arrows. They also trained them to run with a mouthful of water. That's without spilling or swallowing for up to four miles."

"I could use a beer," Bob said.

Someone behind him snorted.

Steve raised his voice over the laughter. "Lalla might want to hear this, you know. As I was saying, they could cover sixty miles on foot, raiding for cattle. It's been said they never took much to horses. They stole 'em, used them to herd the cattle home, then ate them. "

"Injuns," Bob said, "don't talk much as I recall. What'd the daughter say about the old man? He's some kind of shaman, or is that a witch doctor?"

"I guess we'll find out soon enough," Steve said.

This time when Bob groaned, I had to agree with him. The desert before us was a whole lot of cold and rough terrain with enough mesquite to tear off chunks of skin if one were clumsy. Add jumping cholla to the painful stickers and you had an uncomfortable trip.

Hoover surprised me by taking a jog to the east where he kept to a faint trail glimmering lightly against an otherwise sullen landscape.

Steve grunted in relief. "He found a shortcut? Then we'll follow."

Too cold and tired to comment, we picked up our feet, hunched our shoulders against the morning cold and followed the single track as it wound up into the mountains. The sky was now empty of everything but one lone star in the west and the land below us seemed to spread out for miles. A half-hour later, we were face-to-face with the domineering cliffs, their craggy faces still deep in shadow.

"Hear that?" I asked.

Bob jerked his head up, cupped his ears and squeezed his eyes shut. "Donkey and a cow bell a couple of miles away but…"

Steve waived us to be quiet.

I pointed up at the cliffs. "It sounds like someone is drumming," I said. "Think that's him up there? That's good, right, Steve?"

"Yeah, great. He's entertaining himself while he waits for someone to come get him."

"Up there? How're we gonna get him down off that cliff?" Bob asked.

"Not as hard as it looks," Steve said. "The trail is there. Just follow the path to the left and around the rocks. We'll find him."

"Look," Bob said, pointing up the mountain. "Is-is he dancing?"

I followed his pointing finger. I wouldn't have thought there was room for a man to walk around, but from where I stood he looked to be dancing on a pinnacle. An illusion, a trick of light and oddly magical.

The cold was causing my hands to shake so I stuck them back into my pockets to warm them. Heights didn't bother me. It reminded me of flying… well, sort of. A nice enclosed cockpit wasn't a mountain top.

"Should we let him know we're here?" I asked.

"Oh, I'd say he knows." Steve said, turning to our crew.

Steve called the EMTs to put the local hospital on stand by for a helicopter. "Okay. Lalla, me and Bob will go up. If his daughter is right and the ol' boy has dementia, we may have our hands full for an extraction."

Steve zipped up his vest and readjusted the weight in his backpack. "All set, Lalla?"

"Yes," I said, patting the items on my belt and checking again the extra batteries for my radio, the repetition soothing my jittery nerves.

"Then let's get to it." Steve took off, blending into the shadows. I had to jog to keep up. The man was almost sixty, he'd been out here most of the night and he still had the energy to leave the rest of us in the dust. Maybe it was the adrenaline, knowing that our search was almost over. All we had to do was get him off the ledge, down the cliff, get the EMTs to check him over and get him home again.

Steve loped up the trail with us hard on his heels. As we went higher, the going got tougher. Boulders birthed rocks and rocks became slippery shale that made the uphill climb treacherous. I slipped and fell to my knees, cursing at the sharp rocks tearing at my skin. Bob stopped to pull me to my feet and I thanked him, but he just laughed. "I'm sure you'll be able to return the favor someday."

Steve waited for us at a trailhead where a ledge cantilevered over an outcropping of huge boulder. Above us, we heard the old man's shuffling feet keeping time to a drum.

I tilted my head, "What's he singing... is that−?"

Bob chuckled. "Jesus Loves Me? Sure sounds like it. He must've been in Bible school at one time."

Steve shushed us. "We're right under him," he whispered. The drum was now silent but in a weak and reedy voice he started singing the second stanza.

"I think it's best if I go alone," Steve said. "See if I can talk him down. If that doesn't work, I'll come back and we'll split up, take him on both sides."

And if it came to it, the EMTs would sedate him.

Steve ran up the path and disappeared.

I looked down at the valley below. I could hear the team, their voices even at this distance as clear as if I were standing next to them. Of course, the old man heard us coming.

Above us, a voice called. "Hiya!"

We looked up to see a pair of bright black eyes glittering with an unseen light. The elfish, wrinkled face split into a wide grin.

I didn't know how to respond. "Shouldn't Steve be at the ledge by now?"

Bob nudged me. "Say something. It'll distract him until Steve can grab him from behind."

"I'm not so sure about this... what if we spook him?"

"Can't hurt, and he seems interested in you."

The old man's face turned from me to Bob, apparently very interested in our conversation.

Bob tilted his head up and waved. The old man waved back.

"See? He likes you. Go on, say something."

"Me? He waved at you. And what if he doesn't know any English besides the words to *Jesus Loves Me*?"

"Come on, it'll help Steve."

I blew on cold, fisted hands, looked up at the face peering over the ledge. "Uh. Hi there."

He laughed, said something that must have been in his native language and withdrew his head.

"Crap," I said. "I didn't get what he said."

"Apache. I know a little Navajo, but not Apache."

"Wait," I said grabbing Bob's sleeve. "I hear Steve's voice. He's talking to him."

I leaned back, turned on my flashlight and aimed the beam upward.

Bob swatted at the pebbles and feathers cascading onto our helmets. "What the.... ?"

Steve appeared, the light striking him in the face. He threw up his hand, the yellow patch of the Cochise County Search and Rescue Team glinting in the beam. Alarmed that he appeared to be about to go over the ledge, I called to him. "Steve!"

A feather helicoptered down to land on my upturned face. "What the hell is going on?"

"I don't know," Bob said, "but something's wrong. I think we better get up there and find out."

Voices above us rose and fell in argument. Steve consoling, cajoling, the other protesting and suddenly the morning sun burst over the rim of the mountains.

"There!" I said pointing to the silhouetted figure. He was in a brightly beaded and feathered costume but before I could remark on it to Bob, the old man raised his arms over his head and sang. The song, in spite of being in his native language, was enough to give me goose bumps. It was a plaintive cry, but I had no idea if it was for help, or justice or just to make it rain. He stopped for a moment as if to admire the view over the valley, or perhaps he was seeing far into another time.

But then he spread his arms wide, bent his knees, yelled something I couldn't quite hear and leaped into the air.

Feathers did nothing to hold back gravity and his head-long race for the valley floor was quickly met with a violent end. His body bounced once, rolled and finally came to rest against a boulder.

For a few seconds our team stood silent, shock and dismay on their upturned faces until someone yelled and they ran to see if there was any life left in the man to rescue.

Chapter Fourteen:

"I don't know, Caleb," I said, pulling off my dusty hiking boots. "I know it isn't rational, but I could've sworn he said something as he leaped off that ledge and I can't stop thinking that I should've been able to understand it."

Caleb moved one of my pillows from my side of the bed and tucked it behind his back. "I sincerely doubt that you or anyone else could've understood him. He was speaking Apache, wasn't he?"

"I suppose so. But I recognized the words to *Jesus Loves Me*."

"And Steve had no indication that the old guy was going to jump?"

"No. He said he handed the old man his jacket because he was shivering. Later, Steve figured it was just a ruse to distract him and leap off that cliff. Steve feels terrible about it. We all do."

Caleb reached out and pulled me off balance, one boot still dangling from my foot. I fell onto his chest and felt his arms tighten around me.

"It could've been a lot worse," he said, warming my ear with a light kiss.

Caleb would know, since he'd spent the last twenty-three years in law enforcement. First as a deputy, then as sheriff of Stanislaus County in California and now as police chief of Wishbone, Arizona.

"I need a shower," I said, without the energy to back it up.

"Me too," he said, sitting upright with me still encased in his arms. That's what comes of daily exercise in a gym. Me, I just traipse up and down hills all night looking for lost Alzheimer patients.

"Shower?" he asked, nibbling on my dusty ear.

"You're that desperate?"

"No. But I happen to know you're that easy," he said, pulling me out of bed and into the shower.

I have to say, he did a good job of scrubbing my back and the rest of me, and by the time he tucked me into bed and left for work, I felt very clean, very tired and very, very happy.

I was dreaming. It had to be a dream because I was hearing organ music. Hard to hear under water. Water? I looked up. A blue sky. "I could get used to blue sky," my dad said. He should be at his place now. What was he doing, looking down at me as I sat on the bottom of the ocean? The watery image above shifted and morphed into someone else. His face ducked under the water, his black eyes blinked open. He started to speak and drew in a mouthful of water. Choking, he promptly removed his head.

I woke myself up wondering why I could talk under water and he couldn't.

Rolling out of bed, I decided the dream was the result of sleeping late, something I had originally thought of as a decadent luxury that I would indulge in every chance I got. Retired from the aero-ag business meant I was no longer at the beck and call of irritable farmers who expected their crops to be cleared of pests at a moment's notice. I could sleep in as long as I liked. Read or eat crackers and peanut butter in bed. That illusion was quickly snatched away with the day-to-day workload Pearlie and I signed on with Ron Barbour.

Eleven a.m. Uh-oh, Pearlie must've called by now and I slept through it. Deciding I needed coffee before I could face the tongue-lashing I would get from my cousin, I went to the kitchen and found a thermos of hot coffee with a note on it from Caleb; "Hoover looks mighty proud of himself today. He either passed muster last night or he got lucky. Either way, I fed him, gave him a doggy treat and turned off your cell and the land-line so you could sleep."

I gratefully poured myself a cup and invited Hoover to accompany me out to the patio. He yawned, rose from his dog bed and leisurely followed me outside.

Flopping down next to my chair in the shade, he promptly closed his eyes. "You did good last night," I said reaching over and scratching his big ears.

His eyes stayed closed, but his tail tapped the concrete in agreement. "Sorry we didn't save this one, but that's not your fault, is it my good boy?"

The tail thumbed twice. "So what's going to be next for the Hoover? An adventure to be continued?" I picked up my ringing cell phone.

I had to pull the earpiece away from the squawking on the other end.

"Do you know what time it is!" Pearlie yelled.

I yawned. "Hoover and I were on an all-nighter."

Pearlie had a soft spot for the dog. Once upon a time, they had both been strays. "Really? How'd he do?"

"Like the champ he is. He led us right to the man."

"Then it was a successful mission?"

"Yes, except that the object of our rescue waited until we got there to take a header off a cliff." The memory of the old man leaping out into the air only to die from the fall—sure felt like complete failure to me.

"That's tough to take, but I have good news," she said. "We're cleared as suspects in Ron's death. The bad news is that the kid who went to prison for stealing cars from Wade Hamilton has gone missing."

"What? When?"

"That's the interesting part," she said. "I went for that interview with Joey Green and his boss said he didn't come into work yesterday or today."

"He's skipped? Did you call his mother?"

"Sure did."

I thought for a moment. "Is the file on Wade Hamilton still in the office?"

"Lemme look," she said, putting down the phone.

When she picked up again, she seemed oddly calm. "It's gone."

"You're not surprised because...?"

"Because I figured Damian might break in again. I put the original on the back of our evidence board and all he got was an old newspaper clipping of the shooting."

"Why didn't you set the alarm?"

"I fired the alarm company, remember? Besides, I wanted to see how the little rascal would do it. This time he didn't bother to scale the walls, he simply picked the lock."

"Get a new lock for the door."

"We can't afford a locksmith or the alarm company. Besides, I have a better idea."

"What?"

"I've asked his boss to give us a day. All you have to do is find him before his parole officer does."

"Gee thanks. What're you going to do?"

"Have a talk with Damian, of course."

"He's probably at the gym."

"Good. Then this won't take long. Meet me at the office," she said, and hung up.

~~~~~~~~~~

I had just settled into my chair and opened my laptop, ready to start a search for Joey Green when Pearlie walked into the office.

"What did Damian have to say for himself?" I asked.

"Damian, the dear sweet boy that he is, glibly reminded me that *you* told him he could be of help and like I thought he would, he went looking for Joey. Damian's just lucky Joey ran. That guy's already got a nickel of hard time under his belt."

I could see that my cousin was actually enjoying herself. "I gave him a lecture and he's now eager to make it up to us, in any way we want."

"No. Please say you didn't! That kid's a loose cannon! He'll compromise our investigation."

She laughed. "Oh, come on. We could use an extra hand and this way we can keep tabs on the little thief."

Seeing my head swivel five or six times on my neck, Pearlie dropped her smile. "We're already hanging on by a hair. What do we have to lose?"

I ignored the whisper of doubt knocking at my better judgment and gave in. "Okay. Get him in here."

Pearlie opened the door and Damian sauntered in, a wide smile on his mug.

Pearlie went to stand next to our freestanding evidence board, the corked side full of innocuous items: a map of the county, a big calendar and out of date pizza coupons. When she was sure she had his attention, she flipped the six-by-six board over, peeled off the plastic envelope with the original file on Wade Hamilton and waved it under Damian's nose.

"You don't get to waltz into our office and take whatever you like, kid. All you got was some old newsclippings. Certainly not anything that could get you in trouble."

Damian's unrepentant shrug made my fingers itch. I so wanted to slap this kid.

"Take a chair and lose the grin, smart-ass," Pearlie said.

Gee, she sounded just like Ron Barbour. Maybe having an intern of our own to harass might work after all.

"Lalla will show you how to use the computer."

I tossed her a dirty look.

Damian fluttered his lips. "Like I'll hurt your precious computer? You think I'm dumb 'er somethin'?"

Pearlie folded her arms and waited.

I mouthed, *I'll get you for this* and pointed Damian to a chair. "Bring that over here and maybe you'll learn something."

"You said we were going to look for Joey, not do dumb computer stuff."

I lifted a lip and snarled. "Sit! Investigating, as you will soon find out, is research. Sometimes long hours of it, but the payoff can be worth it."

"You actually make money at this shit?"

Pearlie and I looked at each other and, unable to control ourselves, laughed. "So we've been told. Now let's get to work."

I showed Damian how to start with Joey's last known address as a parolee. "What you want to find are his friends, girlfriends and any relatives."

"I know he lived with his mother before he went to prison."

I had to give it to him he had a sharp memory. "Good, but since moms always believe the very best of their children, she's not going to give him up if she thinks he's in trouble, now is she?"

"But he could show up there, couldn't he?"

"Sure. And we'll stake out her house if nothing else turns up. But I want you to start on social media: Facebook, Twitter, Instagram."

Damian's chin lifted defiantly. "I'm down on all that shit."

I shot Pearlie another dirty look. This wasn't going to work; the kid had a chip on his shoulder the size of Kansas. Pearlie had her laptop open and refused to look at me. Got it. I was on my own.

"Okay, but think about this; Joey has been on parole for a year and until yesterday he had a full time job, a home, a mom and probably a girlfriend. You're both local to the area. You may even have mutual friends."

Damian yawned and his eyes drifted over to the skeleton in the corner. Gabby Hayes did say he was bright, good at math and easily bored. I snapped my fingers in front of his face. "Pay attention, and this will go a lot quicker."

His black eyes twinkled like two basalt stones. "I'm just messing with you."

Now he was having fun? We'll see about that. "Fine, fine. I'm going to leave this picture of Joey next to the computer for comparison. Go on your socials, mention that you're taking a break from training for American Ninja Warrior to catch up with friends, okay? Ask what's new with them. Do not mention his name to anyone. Do a search for his real name, then search for any nicknames he might have. You have a nickname; use that to your advantage. At the very least you'll get some new friend requests. If you see a nickname, ask what their real name is and what they do. He may lie, but that's okay. Post pictures of yourself training. He may post pictures of himself. If it's not him, then move on. I'm hoping that you can lure him into friending you because of your training for ANW. He may claim to live in Fairbanks, Alaska, but he'll have his picture either as part of his profile or gallery photos."

"Anything else?" he asked, his hands poised over the keyboard.

"If you get stumped or reach a dead end, let me know."

His response to that idea was a loud belch. And that was meant to annoy me? If I could put up with Ron Barbour's antics for three years, I could handle this kid. Out of the corner of my eye, I watched his fingers fly. I'd forgotten that kids these days grew up with computers and if Damian was half the computer whiz he said he was, I could relax.

Pearlie gestured her approval with a thumbs-up. I shuddered. Every time someone gave a big thumbs-up, something bad happened. I could only hope this time I was wrong.

"What's next?" I asked.

"We need to find a stoolie."

I thought for a minute. "A disgruntled employee would do it and I think I know just the person. She used to be Wade's bookkeeper, but she's now a hairdresser at Suzi's."

"Suzi?"

"You remember Darlene, don't you? Married to Wishbone's two-timing, wife-beating police chief?"

"Oh, *that* Darlene. Is she still doing your hair?"

"Darlene sold her shop to Suzi and moved to Phoenix, but you'd know that if you didn't run all the way to Tucson to get your hair done."

"I write the trip off as part of my business mileage," she said, primping her artfully blended blonde locks. "Well, at least I did, until Ron sucked up all the business."

"Patience, dear cousin. First we get an arrest for Ron's murderer, find Damian's dad's killer and if we're still in business in a week we'll hunt up some new business."

"Since you go to Suzi, I presume you want the honor of going there now?"

"Might as well," I said, grabbing my purse and pausing at the door. "What're you going to do while I'm gone?"

"Go over Ron's old bank statements. Look for more clients he cheated. You never know, we might find someone else we can lean on for information. Bring lunch back for us, will you?"

"Because research always makes you hungry, right? I'll pick something up on the way back." I had one foot out the door when I turned back and said, "Don't forget, Pearlie, Ron was murdered because he also leaned on someone."

Chapter Fifteen:

I pulled into the last parking spot at Suzi's beauty shop, hopped out and walked inside.

Suzi had one client under the dryer and another woman's head over the sink.

I eyed her tattooed bicep, checking the last in a long list of names. Yep. No ink crossing out her latest boyfriend, so she might be feeling generous today.

She saw me looking and laughed. "He's not on my shit list yet. What's up?"

"I wanted to talk to Emily, if she's here."

Suzi looked around the room. "She must be out back having a cigarette. What'd you want her for?"

I pretended I didn't hear the question and took the back door exit.

Sure enough, Wade's ex-bookkeeper was sitting alone at the patio table, reading a fashion magazine. She looked up as I approached, squinting through a haze of cigarette smoke.

Ron always said to ease into the subject when interviewing a nervous witness, so I pulled up a chair and with a smile in my voice, said, "Those things will stunt your growth."

She closed the magazine and looked me over. "I suppose you quit before it stunted yours, right? What're you, six feet?"

"Minus a couple of inches," I said.

The crow's feet at her eyes tightened as she tracked my face down to my hands, something I'd seen battered wives do as an automatic reflex to possible attack. I said, "Suzi does my hair and I'm a friend of Darlene's."

"Oh? I got hired after Darlene moved to Denver."

She was testing me. "Denver? No, I think it was Phoenix."

"Oh, yeah, right. Phoenix," she said, visibly relaxing.

"I helped Darlene when her husband was murdered."

Emily stubbed out her cigarette and licked her lips. "I read about it in the papers. You're the private investigator Suzi talks about, aren't you?"

She was at that tipping point, warming to the idea that I might be helpful but also fearful of the outcome.

"I'm wondering if there isn't something we can do for each other, Emily."

She chewed on her lip while her eyes darted from the door of the shop to her pack of cigarettes.

I mentally counted to ten. Guilty or not, nerves usually drove witnesses and suspects to close the gap of silence, especially when there was an offer on the table. The only types I've met who could tolerate the sound of quiet were professional poker players and sociopaths. If she didn't bite, I'd leave my card and walk away, hoping she'd reconsider.

I did a mental countdown. *Ten, nine, eight...*

She cracked at seven. "What do you want?"

"I'm guessing that the change from Wade Hamilton's bookkeeper to hair stylist was not voluntary. Did Wade refuse to give you a reference? Did he threaten to accuse you of embezzlement?"

Emily's gasp told me I'd hit a sore spot. "It's not true!"

"I wouldn't be here if I thought it was."

"Then what do you want?"

"Well, for one thing, I have good news. Wade Hamilton is on a short list of suspects in a recent murder investigation and I presume that you'd like to see him in prison. If not for murder, then at least for the burglaries he and Joey Green committed."

"You're talking about Ron Barbour's murder, right? You think Wade did it? Killed Ron?"

"We should talk about that."

She crushed out the cigarette and stood. "I tried that once. I was fired without references and threatened. Do you know that the smug bastard sends me a sympathy card once a year? And me, with a disabled husband at home. I'm sorry, but I can't help you."

I grabbed at her hand as she passed. "Who did you talk to? Was it someone in the police or sheriff's department? Times have changed. I can get you protection, Emily."

She jerked her hand out of my grasp. "If you think you can get to Wade Hamilton, you're nuts. He's got friends in high places and I've got no one but myself and my Henry." Her eyes teared up. "Henry had a stroke when he was forty. Forty. He still can't talk right or walk without his cane and he sure can't work. We struggle just to get by every month." With a sob, she threw up a hand, striking the air between us. "Just... just leave me alone!"

With her head down, she ran for the steps and fled back into Suzi's shop.

I sat where I was for a few more minutes thinking about my conversation with Wade Hamilton's former bookkeeper. Emily must've confided what she knew about Wade's involvement with Joey's burglaries to someone in the police or sheriff's department. That person then told Wade, who fired her and proceeded to send ominous sympathy cards every year to remind her to keep quiet. If I were in her position, I doubt I would talk either. Emily was going to keep her secrets until either she died or Wade Hamilton was put behind bars.

~~~~~~~~~~

With black summer clouds threatening to burst any minute, I trotted up the outside stairs and into our office.

Pearlie had her feet propped up on Ron's desk, her laptop open.

"You forgot our lunch," she said, her eyes on the screen.

"I'm sorry, I forgot the time. I got caught up talking to Wade Hamilton's ex-bookkeeper."

"It better be worth it. That kid ate up my lunch allowance into next month."

"He's in training, remember? I'll make it up to you."

"You better. I don't have a husband with a regular income and a house that's paid for."

Now she was working me for sympathy. "If you can't pay your rent, we have a spare couch."

"Ew-w-w. I'm not that poor."

"Since we're talking about men, how was your date with the trainer from the gym?"

Pearlie's mouth twitched. "Just because a man has *Genius* printed on his T-shirt, doesn't mean he is one."

I grinned. "Not hunky enough to ignore his IQ, huh?"

"Not if he was wrapped in bacon and came with his own trust fund."

I laughed and swiped up her last cold French fry. "What happened to the guy with the Prius? That sounded like a safe bet."

"Yeah, how dangerous can a guy be if he's driving a Prius, right? Turns out the Prius is registered to his wife."

"I thought we agreed that you'd ask *the* question before you accepted a date?"

"Must've slipped my mind. Besides, it was our first and last date. Anyways, I can't possibly think about dating again until we solve Damian's case, find Ron's killer and get our P.I. licenses."

When she said things like this, I remembered how close we were to losing it all. At least I had some news and told her about my conversation with Emily.

Pearlie's feet dropped off the desk. "Then Wade Hamilton was in cahoots with a cop?"

"Or a deputy sheriff and I can see why Ian was so adamant that we keep his list to ourselves. By the way, where's Damian?"

"Ate his lunch, all of yours and left for the gym."

"Did you get any work out of him at all?"

"Oh yes. He found the girlfriend. I had to wrestle the darn kid to the ground to keep him from snatching my cuffs and running after Joey."

I would've paid good money to see that, but then Pearlie did tend to exaggerate. "You have to admire his enthusiasm."

"I put the brakes on that by offering to let him accompany *you* on the stakeout tonight."

Nights are when most skips come home to roost and Pearlie was betting that Joey Green was no different than any other jailbird. But I didn't see how bringing in Joey Green was going to help our case and besides, I had a husband to go home to at night. "Why don't we let the police pick up Joey Green?"

"No can do," she said. "Joey's mom is desperate to keep her boy out of prison. She's offered to pay our fee plus expenses if we can find him before his boss reports him AWOL. Besides, Damian thinks you're a great teacher."

She was right. This could be a quick hundred dollars in our fading bank account. "Fine, fine," I said. "But I'm taking your taser."

"I understand completely," she said, grinning. "Just don't let Damian see it, or he'll want to take it out for a spin. How're you going to do it?"

"Pizza, of course."

She looked at her watch. "Good. You'll explain the play to Damian, then? He'll be here any minute."

Thinking back to all the nonsense he's put us through, I said, "If he shows at all."

"I'll bet you five dollars he will. I'm taking the files home. If you find Joey Green, push him to turn state's evidence on Wade Hamilton."

~~~~~~~~~~~~

Damian arrived at five minutes before five. He threw his backpack onto a chair and ran fingers through his recently showered curls.

"You ready to roll?" I asked.

"Where's the pizza?"

"That's one of our methods to getting skips to come to the door. But, if you behave yourself, I'll buy you pizza after, okay?"

"I guess," he said, with a shrug. "So what's the first thing we do?"

"We order pizza, of course."

I swiveled around in my chair, picked up the phone and punched in the number for Papa John's Pizza.

"I'd like to order a large with everything on it," I said. "Yes please, delivered." I recited the girlfriend's house number and street. "My boyfriend already called it in? Gee, that's great. I work in Sierra Vista but I'm on my way home now, what time will you deliver? Six? Thanks."

I hung up and grinned. "Saddle up, Geronimo, we've got work to do."

Damian popped out of his chair and slammed out of the door before I could mention that he didn't have to run.

He was waiting for me on the sidewalk. "Hurry up, we're going to miss the delivery," he said. "Where's your car?"

I had to lean over my knees to catch my breath. Darn kid. All that unnecessary energy was beginning to annoy me. "You came in a car, didn't you? We'll go in yours. You can write up an expense report and give it to our client."

"Okay. Wait. You said, client. You mean my mom, don't you? I don't know. My uncle Ian supports me while I'm training, but I don't think my mom will like me charging her for extra gas."

"We have a different client," I said. "Someone who doesn't want Joey screwing up and losing parole." If I guessed right, Joey's mother was living off a bribe Wade Hamilton paid to keep the mom quiet and Joey in prison. It was only fair that we put Damian's gas on our expense report, especially if we got Joey to roll on his former boss.

We took Damian's beat up old blue truck out to Benson, found the girlfriend's apartment and parked close enough to see if anyone went in or out of the unit, but not so close that we could be spotted.

Five minutes later, pizza delivery rolled in. I hopped out and told Damian to stay in the truck. Naturally, he didn't listen and got out to follow me.

I put a hand on his chest to stop him. "Lesson number one. One person per job. Two people show up and Joey will think we're the cops. Now get back in the truck and wait."

"No way. If he worked for Wade Hamilton, he knows who killed my dad."

"Damian, what went on with Joey Green and Wade Hamilton was years after the shooting. It's his testimony against Wade that could mean the difference between getting Wade to opt for a plea on your father's murder or not. Now will you please go sit in the truck?"

When he reluctantly agreed, I trotted over to the delivery car and retrieved the pizza before the kid could get out of his car.

But before I could get to the apartment, Damian grabbed the wide flat pizza box out of my hand and pushed me aside. I stuck out my foot and tripped him. One minute he was headed for the ground and the next he twisted around so that he landed on his back, the pizza box held aloft, just asking me to accept it.

"Well, that was stupid," I said, removing the box from his hand.

Holding it securely between both hands, I started out again for the door to the apartment.

Even while I was still shaking my head at his silly maneuver, he tackled me around the knees. I slammed into the ground like a tree felled in the forest, and the last thing I remember was the distinct smell of pepperoni pizza.

I awoke to hear Damian calmly explaining his position on gun control.

I groaned and reaching up, felt an icepack and the hand that held it. I looked up and a wide-eyed girl with stringy blond hair was staring at me.

"Where's Damian?" I asked the girl.

She pointed to Damian standing next to a young man in jeans and a T-shirt tied to a kitchen chair.

"Wha... what's going on?"

The girl breathed deeply and patted a spot over her heart. "Thank God, you're alive. He said we'd go to prison if you died."

"I'll live." I handed her the ice pack and addressed the burly young man in the chair. "I presume you're Joey Green?"

"Yes, ma'am."

I nodded and wobbled to my feet. Hanging onto the edge of the couch I said, "Damian, can I talk to you outside, please?"

Closing the door behind me, I pushed a finger into his chest and promptly felt dizzy.

Damian grabbed me by the shoulder. "You okay?"

"I will be. As soon as I kick your butt." But still a bit woozy, my words sort of lost their punch.

"You should thank me," he said. "I know the pizza guy from the gym. He's also a friend of Joey's. I got in there and cuffed Joey before he could warn him."

"You used my cuffs? He could get a lawyer and have you arrested for illegal restraint."

"Uncle Ian says I can do a private citizen's arrest any-time I want. Besides, you're not legal either and Joey is all set to talk. All you gotta do is ask him."

My head hurt and I smelled like pepperoni pizza, but other than that I was fine and considering that Joey was tied to a chair, he seemed to be completely relaxed.

"You have to uncuff him, Damian. We're not here to arrest him; we're here to give him the good news about his former boss."

"I did that already," he said. "I told him everything; that you knew Joey got a bum deal when he was sent to prison and that you needed his testimony against Wade Hamilton. Do I still get pizza?"

Okay, so it hadn't gone exactly as planned and Damian was still a pain in the ass but I got what I came for, didn't I?

"Sure," I said. "I'll pick you up a whole one on the way home."

Chapter Sixteen:

Damian's pizza was half eaten before I dropped him at his uncle's house. I congratulated Ian on his nephew's sleuthing abilities, didn't mention the kid tackling me in the parking lot or that he'd stolen my cuffs to use on Joey Green.

On the way home, I called Pearlie, gave her the update and reassuring her that I still had her taser, I went back to reading street signs; Apache, Navajo, Yaqui, Cochise and even a Geronimo. Damian's middle name and his nickname at the gym was Geronimo. His uncle Ian named one of his champion quarter horses Geronimo. What was it about the name Geronimo that made me think I was missing something?

Was that what the old Apache yelled when he leaped to his death? Now, that would make sense; WW II Rangers yelled Geronimo when they jumped out of airplanes, didn't they? But somehow, I thought it was three words, but what? I shook off this latest round of obsessive behavior and aimed my Jeep for home.

Happy to see Caleb's SUV parked next to our house, I pounded some of the dust from my boots onto the welcome mat and opened the front door. "Helloooo," I called. "I'm home!"

He was on the patio, stretched out on a chaise lounge. He turned at the sound of my voice and held up his empty glass.

I grabbed the pitcher of iced tea from the fridge, a glass for me, nudged open the French doors and set the icy pitcher onto a small table between the two chaise lounges. With a deep sigh, I looked down before sitting and saw that Hoover had claimed my spot.

Caleb laughed and swatted at the dog. "Go lay down on your own bed, you mutt."

"I presume you're talking to Hoover, not me, right?"

He grinned. "Unless you've changed your name when I wasn't looking."

I refilled his iced tea leaned back and tried to relax. "You're home early."

"I have some news," he said, sitting up.

My earlier good mood evaporated. "Bad news, I suppose?"

"No, no. I'm pleased to say that Andy Sokolov's tenure as child molester was a huge overstatement. He was fifteen and babysitting a seven-year-old terror. When he'd had enough of her shenanigans, he put her over his knee and spanked her bottom."

"Well that doesn't sound so awful, but I suppose the parents reported him."

"He got a court ordered psychologist and probation."

"I'm glad to hear it. I know how much you like and respect Andy. Wait a minute. Caleb, if he was under eighteen, his record would've been sealed. How did you get this information?"

"I asked him."

"Oh, Caleb! You know we aren't supposed to let any of Ian's suspects know we were looking at them."

"I'll get to that in a minute. The other news is that Wade Hamilton's twenty-foot fishing boat was found abandoned at Patagonia Lake today. The park ranger wasn't surprised to see the boat on the water, but all day without moving from the same spot got him worried. Wade's truck is there with a day use permit stamped for day before yesterday. Except for an empty whiskey bottle in the bottom of the boat, there was no sign of him."

"Don't they usually check the day use tickets at the end of the day?" I asked.

"The ranger on duty for the last couple of days has been reprimanded."

"So, where is he?" I asked.

"Santa Cruz County Search and Rescue sent their scuba team to scour the bottom. As soon as Ian Tom found out it was Wade's boat, he called me. I've been out at the lake most of today, but so far," Caleb said, looking at his watch, "no one has called to say they've found him."

"Why did you tell Andy he was on the list?"

"It just didn't seem fair to Andy, so I asked. He confirmed his alibi with a printed itinerary. Twenty people can vouch for his whereabouts during the hours someone killed Ron Barbour."

I wasn't happy about it, but if Caleb's trust in his best friend took a turn for the worse, no one would be quicker to make it right than my husband.

I mentally cringed. I'd just scolded Caleb for letting one of Ian's suspects in on our case, when Damian's inept attempt to corner Joey Green may have had something to do with Wade's disappearance. I would have to accept some of the responsibility, but since I'd promised not to withhold anything from him, I told him about Damian and finding Joey Green.

Caleb looked shocked at the notion that I should trust the kid. "Damian broke into your office again and you reward him with a job?"

"We're short-handed," I said, waving my hands around in the air. "It was either recruit him or he'd continue being a nuisance. It's Wade's ex-bookkeeper that's the holdout."

"Why?"

"She's terrified of him."

"What does he have on her?"

"His culpability in the burglaries with Joey Green. But when she tried to tell someone in law enforcement, they told Wade. Wade fired her and has continued to threaten her with annual reminders in the form of sympathy cards sent to her home. She won't talk because she doesn't trust anyone."

"Is she sure it was an officer of the law? Lalla, we haven't had a problem in the department since Abel Dick and that was the first incident with Cochise County's law enforcement in twenty years."

Deputy Abel Dick had been sucked into a murderous scheme to defraud landowners of their property as well as covering up a murder. Unfortunately, his redemption came too late.

I hopped off the chaise and paced the length of the patio. "Wade's bookkeeper didn't actually say who it was, only that it was someone she thought she could trust. I assumed it was a cop or a deputy. Maybe a lawyer?"

"Did you get a sense that she'd talk if she knew Wade is missing?" Caleb asked.

I looked at my watch. "Suzi and Emily usually work until seven."

He sucked down the last of his iced tea. "Suzi's shop is in Wishbone, right? Let me put Hoover in the house with his supper and I'll join you in the Jeep."

~~~~~~~~~~

On the way to see Emily, I got an earful from Caleb about Damian. "He's too young, too foolish. You can't trust him not to take matters in his own hands."

"Damian is willful," I said, "but he's right about one thing; the sheriff's department won't reopen his father's case without proof and he's determined to get it."

Caleb hummed, but otherwise didn't offer any more opinions for the fifteen-minute ride to Suzi's.

Turning off the engine, he said, "Ready?"

"Yes," I said.

I let Caleb, as police chief, break the news to her that Wade was missing and presumed dead.

Grabbing a Kleenex out of the box on the counter, she blew her nose and with a trembling smile, said, "Sorry. It's just after all these years…. You really think he could be dead, Chief Stone?"

"Or, he's slipped across the border into Mexico," Caleb said. "Either way, I doubt you have to worry about Wade Hamilton bothering you again."

She huffed out a bitter laugh. "And there I was wondering why I hadn't gotten an anniversary card from him."

"Has he tried to get in touch with you recently, Emily?" I asked.

"No and I thought it odd, because I'm always a wreck about now wondering what spiteful trick he'll use this year. But if he's dead… "

"I have more good news. Even if he is found alive, Joey Green is now willing to testify against him."

"I can't believe it. I'm free. Oh God, I can't wait to tell Henry."

"Are you now willing to tell us who it was you confided in about Wade Hamilton?" Caleb asked.

"I'm glad to finally be able to talk about it," she said, looking directly at me. "It was Ron Barbour. He convinced me that he was working with the police on the theft ring."

"I'm so sorry, Emily," I said, chagrined that the woman thought I might be part of Ron's deceit. "I had no idea, but then the last few days have been a real eye-opener on my former business partner's bad behavior."

At my words the lines around her mouth visibly relaxed. "You too, huh?"

"We'll talk about it someday, but for now is there anything else you'd like to share about Wade?"

"One other thing," she said. "I saw the hefty check Wade made out to Joey's mom. I don't know if you'll be able to prove it, but I think it was in exchange for Joey's silence on Wade's participation in the theft of those cars."

"Thank you for your time, Emily. I'll have a detective get in touch with you later today," Caleb said.

In the car again, Caleb pried apart my fisted hands. "Hungry?"

"Not really. I guess we have to add snitch to the growing list of reprehensible behavior for Ron Barbour."

"You'll feel better after you eat," he said, putting the Jeep in gear and heading up Tombstone Canyon Road to Screaming Banshee's Pizza. Being close to the county courthouse, it was also his favorite place for lunch when he had to go to court.

Nik was leaning over the bar, working on a new menu with the owner. When she saw me, she rounded the bar to give me one of her fearfully strong hugs. "Baby girl! Where you been?"

Since Nik topped my five-foot-ten by two inches she could call me baby girl and give me huge hugs anytime she wanted.

"Oh, an' look who you brought. How you doin', Chief Stone?" she asked, playfully punching him on the arm. "I haven't seen you in a couple of days."

Caleb smiled politely and managed not to rub his shoulder until Nik excused herself for work.

"That woman packs a mean punch," he said, rubbing the spot.

I laughed at him, feeling somewhat better about this case since giving Emily the news that she was forever free of Wade Hamilton.

We found a seat outside and when we ordered, Caleb said, "I almost forgot, Ian Tom got a judge to allow wire taps on the three suspects'."

"In case Wade is still alive and decides to call home?"

"It could happen, you know."

"What about Jesse Jefferson?"

Caleb looked away. "I tried, but Ian won't make an exception for Jesse just because he's our favorite pastor."

"If he's wrong, his career as county sheriff could be on the line," I said.

"Censured, reprimanded, or just not win his next election," Caleb said. He was reminding me that the job of county sheriff was an elected law enforcement position and maybe the reason why Ian Tom gave us the dubious honor of investigating three respectable men.

Unable to come up with a solution to this problem we gave ourselves over to enjoying the food and the evening's entertainment. Tonight, Becky and her partner played a few tunes. Becky had a wonderful singing voice and Caleb and I leaned back, ordered another round of beer and left thoughts of criminals behind us for the rest of the evening.

Chapter Seventeen:

The next morning I met Pearlie at the office with breakfast sandwiches and plenty of good coffee.

"Oh, thank God! I'm starved," she said, grabbing a sandwich. "How'd it go last night? Joey give you any trouble, or did he fold like a weak card in a high stakes poker game?"

I smiled at my cousin's reference to poker. "Joey folded easily enough. He's agreed to spill everything he knows about Wade Hamilton. Oh, and his mother came through with the check. Did the insurance company pay us yet?"

"Yes," she said. "And with the check you got last night, we can pay our bills until the end of the month. Mentioning insurance companies, Detective Hutton called. Good job on getting Wade's bookkeeper to crack. The detective figures the insurance fraud alone will get Wade a one way ticket to prison."

"If he's alive."

"Detective Hutton said the divers were called off yesterday. Wade Hamilton better be dead," she said, "'cause if he ain't, I'm gonna want a piece out of his hide for killing Ron."

"You'd rather have Ron back?" I asked. "You do get that the man has ruined our livelihood, don't you?"

"Not yet, he hasn't and we still have his funeral to attend. Just a minute," she said, picking up the newspaper. "Lemme find the notice."

"With the way things're going," I said. "Maybe we should skip his funeral. What if we run into his exes?"

"We'll sit in the back and make a quick exit," she said, scanning the list for Ron's funeral.

After this weekend, we could expect to get a notice from an attorney representing the two ex-wives, along with a phone call or a registered letter telling us that Ron's P.I. license had been revoked. Squeezed out of business by the state and Ron's two ex-wives expecting the balance of our contract made for a pretty grim looking future. I counted on my fingers—today was Thursday. We had Friday and the weekend. Thank God government offices were closed on the weekends. We had less than a week to solve Ron's murder, resolve Damian's case, collect the money his mother owed us and prostrate ourselves before the State Board and beg for our license. I felt dizzy just thinking about it.

Pearlie slapped a hand on the folded out newspaper. "Well, well, well. Guess we're going to Ron's funeral after all."

I looked up. "Huh?"

"You'll never guess where the funeral is going to be held today—Pastor Jefferson's church in Wishbone."

"I doubt Ron ever saw the inside of any church, much less Jesse's," I said, "but one of his family members could've requested it."

"You know the pastor?"

"Caleb and I attend Christmas and Easter Sunday services there and I have to say that they're wonderful. He's got a terrific choir, his sermons are upbeat, and he's managed to attract and keep a mixed race congregation."

"Charismatic, huh?" she asked. "Or working on redemption because he shot a man in the back?"

Pearlie and I had gone around and around on Ian's addition of the pastor as a suspect. Money problems was all Ian would say, but we couldn't find anything. Not in the files Caleb gave us on Jesse's finances, or anything negative from his parishioners. Everyone liked Jesse, me included. Still, it lay like an overcooked egg and it was beginning to smell bad.

"I don't know," I said. "He preaches the gospel, jokes with the kids, does couples counseling and makes time for anyone who asks for help."

Pearlie closed the newspaper. "We're going to Ron's funeral, but just in case there's trouble, leave your police chief husband at home."

"What about my dad? He always enjoys a good funeral."And the receptions and the free food and the lonely widows—though lately he seemed to have his hands full dodging the B&B owner trying to corral him into marrying her.

"How fast can he run?" she asked, tipping her head in question.

"Seriously?"

"His two ex-wives will be all over us like stink on a hound dog. Whadya think they're going to say when we tell 'em we're broke?"

"Okay, no dad, no Caleb—got it."

We would sit in the back so we'd be the first ones out of the door. Then we'd drift over to our car where we'd discreetly photograph the attendees and make a quick getaway before Ron's ex-wives saw us. That was the plan anyway.

I had enough time to go home, feed Hoover, answer a couple of phone calls and call Caleb to tell him where I was going this morning.

"You don't want to go, do you?" I asked, hoping he was too busy to attend Ron's funeral.

"No thanks," he said with a laugh. "One member of this family associated with Ron Barbour should be enough. Say hi to Detective Hutton for me. Oh, and please be careful."

"Careful? Yeah sure," I said, but keeping my voice steady and confident wasn't so easy. "Ron's two crazy ex-wives will be gunning for us. Why on earth would any man in his right mind marry and divorce one woman only to then marry her sister? Velma and Zelma. Shoot, even their names sound like trouble."

"I was thinking more in the line of news people," he said with a smile. "They'll be after you for a story. You two being his *employees*."

"Thanks for the reminder, but we're going to sit in the back and do that low profile thing Ian keeps talking about."

Ron just had to let everyone think he paid us to work for him. What a couple of chumps we turned out to be.

Caleb chuckled and just before he hung up said, "Oh, you'll want to hear this; Ron Barbour's autopsy said he was struck by a blunt instrument on the back of his head, but died from smoke inhalation. Call me after the funeral and tell me if anything interesting happens."

I was about to leave when my dad drove up and tooted his horn.

"Hi Dad," I said, pulling up next to his driver's side window. "Are you going to the mine?"

"I'm taking Rafe and his cousins their lunch. Those boys're making good progress clearing out all that rock from the mine."

"Do your miner friends have any more ideas on who did it?" I asked.

Something passed across my dad's eyes. He cut the engine on his Jeep and got out to lean on my open window. "Nothing concrete, but...."

"Spit it out Dad, I've got a funeral to go to."

"Ron Barbour's, huh? You sure you want to do that? Seems to me he had more enemies than friends."

I was running late, but if my father was working up to something, I needed to pay attention. "Go on," I said, turning off the motor. "Tell me what's on your mind."

He fidgeted for a minute, then said, "You know I think the world of Caleb, respect his abilities as a lawman to no end and I wouldn't want you to think anything bad about his opinions, 'cause we've all got 'em...."

"Yes, yes and he's as perfect in every way, as you've told me about a thousand times, so what is it this time?"

"I just wanted to remind you that I once thought my good friend Burdell Smith wouldn't abuse our thirty-year friendship. Yet, he used me to settle his debt with the Feds and that one lie let loose a whole passel of trouble on our family."

Burdell Smith owed the IRS big time and thought if he took that deal with the feds, nobody was going to get hurt. He lied to me about a pilot's credentials, which got him killed and led a vicious Las Vegas hit man to our doorstep.

"You think Andy Sokolov lied to Caleb?" I asked.

Dad pulled on his ear, a sure sign that what he had to tell me could be up for interpretation. "Well now, that's where it gets complicated. You know my friend, Gabby Hayes. She says Andy's father was a miner."

"Where're you going with this Dad?"

"Andy's dad was a blaster too, taught his son every-thing he knew about charges and non-els."

"So Andy knew how to use explosives and conduits. My God, Dad, what would be his motive?"

"You're going to have to decide that for yourself, but Gabby's best friend was a social worker for the county. The friend told Gabby there was a woman who tried to get so-cial services to investigate Andy Sokolov for sexually abus-ing her fifteen-year-old daughter."

"But no charges? Were they dropped? How long ago did this happen?"

"All's she said was that the woman moved to Tucson and no charges were ever filed."

It wasn't much of a lead, but I wasn't about to discredit it. Not since Ian put sexual abuse next to Andy Sokolov's name. "Have you got anything else? A name?"

He pulled a piece of paper out of his pocket and, as if reluctant to hand off more trouble to me, released it into my open palm. "Margaret Painter is her name and this is her phone number. Gabby said to tell you that she's expecting your phone call."

~~~~~~~~~~~

I met Pearlie at the office and on the way to Ron's fu-neral, told her about a possible lead I wanted to follow up on Andy Sokolov.

"That could be dicey," Pearlie said. "You want me to interview her?"

Pearlie had had her own dealings with sexual abuse and though I didn't doubt intentions, I thought I might be more objective. "The woman is expecting me, but thanks."

"When are you going to see her?" she asked.

"Sometime this afternoon," I said, looking at my watch.

She flopped down into her chair, shuffled through the newspaper and held up the front page for me to see. "What the hell is this?"

The front page of the Sierra Vista Herald said, *New break in the Miracle Faith Church Shootout* with a picture of deputies around Wade's abandoned fishing boat.

"Come on, Pearlie, what's the first rule of any investigator? Turn up the heat on possible suspects with subterfuge and misdirection. "

"All it says is that the sheriff's department is close to solving an old murder. But they aren't, are they?"

"Not any more than they were yesterday, "I said. "With Wade Hamilton presumed dead and Ron Barbour murdered, Sheriff Tom got a judge to sign for a wiretap on all three suspects."

"That's good news, but I don't suppose Ian will tell us anything."

"Caleb will," I said. I'd been good on my promise to share with him, so he'd better.

~~~~~~~~~~~

We accepted the folded program from a deacon and entered the sanctuary. The church wasn't exactly packed, but then I didn't expect Ron had many friends. His two ex-wives and four teenage children sat in the front row. About twenty people were sprinkled here and there, but not close enough so that one could hold any kind of conversation.

Sierra Vista homicide detective Brock Hutton passed by, nodded and kept going up the aisle until he found an empty pew. I didn't want to talk to him either. If he was here, it meant he didn't have a suspect in custody. Good. We still had a chance to find Ron's killer before he did.

Seeing there was no flower covered coffin, I assumed that the widows wasted no time in getting Ron cremated.

I recognized a couple of our clients. They must have thought enough of our former boss to show up. Or they just wanted to make sure he was dead. Either way, here were readymade clients and a golden opportunity. I nudged Pearlie. "Did you bring your business cards?"

Her head was on her chest, her program open in her lap and there was that telltale sound of snoring. "What's the point of being here if you can't stay awake?"

"Don't fuss," she muttered, moving around on the hard bench for a more comfortable position. "I had a long night."

"Doing what—or should I say, whom?"

I don't know how many times we'd both done all-night surveillance, taking turns getting a little shut-eye when and where we could. But since Detective Hutton came up in the conversation this morning, my guess is that's where she was until the wee hours of the morning. Yep. There she went again. Eyes closed, head dropped onto her chest and a kind of whirring sound that was definitely a Pearlie snore. I let her snooze. We could speak to the clients after the service.

Pastor Jefferson reminded us that we are all sinners and that Jesus forgives. Dang it. And here I was hoping Ron was somewhere hot and miserable, the rat-bastard. He had left us with not one, but two murders to solve, and our future careers as legitimate P.I.'s seriously in jeopardy.

The pastor's sermon ended, a hymn was sung, and Pearlie woke up with a snort.

"Oh good, you're awake. Let's go," I said, nudging her to get a move on.

We waited in the shade of a big old oak tree, holding our cameras at waist height and shooting pictures of the mourners stumbling out of the sanctuary and into the bright sunlight. Detective Hutton blinked at us, hesitated, stuck his hands in his pockets and sauntered in the opposite direction. Ah. I was right. I would've ribbed her about it, but two of Ron's former clients were coming our way.

"You got your business cards?" I asked Pearlie. "Good. There's Jameson Insurance from Tucson. Get us a meeting with his boss next week. I'll take the one from Sierra Vista."

"I thought we were here to look for suspects?"

I hesitated. Possible suspects against future business? "Wade Hamilton and Andy Sokolov are no shows and we need the business. I'll meet you at the car."

The insurance man from Sierra Vista looked at my card and smiled. "You're the LB on our reports, aren't you? Ron never said, but we always thought the hired help was doing most of the work."

I would've corrected him on our status as hired help, but I could do that later. "Gee, thanks! All we're asking is that you consider using our services."

He stuck out his hand. "I'll be happy to recommend you to my boss."

I thanked him and turned for the car, a grin on my face and my step lighter for the first time since Ron's death. Maybe things would turn out after all.

My euphoria lasted for about two more steps until a hand grabbed my arm. I turned to face the last two people I wanted to see today. Velma and Zelma, hands on wide hips, sour expressions on their vivid red lips. Wasn't it enough that I had to listen to their squabbling over who got their check first? Maybe Ron hadn't gone from one to the other so much as he simply gave up and gave in. I bet they were sorry now.

"We know you weren't *just* his employees," Velma sneered.

"Yeah, who do you think you are anyways?" Zelma added, looking me up and down.

Who did I think I was? I started to tell her that we were his business partners... then I did a mental head smack. We had it all wrong. The sisters didn't know about the contract, they thought we were fooling around with Ron. As Pearlie would say, *Ewww!*

Pearlie and I were convinced it was simply Ron's big ego that made him want to keep our partnership a secret, when the truth was he didn't want his exes to know he was cutting them loose. I had another thought—if they didn't know we still owed him his final payment, did we really want to tell them? I almost laughed. Trust Ron to teach all of us the finer points of bad behavior. No, no. I couldn't let the lie stand. It was hard to swallow, but better now than later.

"I wasn't his employee, Zelma. Pearlie and I were his business partners."

"Whadya mean, business partners? Ron said—"

As far as the two women were concerned, we were merely there to warm his lap? Double *ewww.*

"Sorry to break it to you but Ron lied a lot. Three years ago, we answered his ad. He wanted to sell his business. We had experience, but not the kind that the state of Arizona would accept to get our P.I. licenses. We struck a deal. He got a down payment and we split the expenses and profits. After three years of indentured servitude, we'd give him his last check and he'd write us a letter of recommendation to the state of Arizona. He didn't tell you any of this?"

Zelma put her hand to her forehead and groaned. I knew just how she felt.

It took Velma two seconds before all the pieces clicked into place and then her mouth rounded into multiple zeros. "How much did he get? I mean before he was killed?"

"Twenty thousand."

"No!" Seeing that I was telling the truth, the two women looked at each other, triumph glittering in their eyes. "Then we get what you owed him."

"Sorry, no. We insisted on a watertight contract drawn up by a lawyer. In case one of us died, the remaining partners became sole heirs to the business."

"He did no such thing!" Zelma cried.

In any other circumstance, I would've felt sorry for them. Velma patted her sister's shoulder, all the while considering me through narrowed eyes. If I stayed one minute longer the two of them would start peppering me with questions and Pearlie and I were on a deadline.

I heard Pearlie come up behind me and ask, "What's going on here?"

Seeing an out, I took Pearlie's arm and towed her for the car, opened my door, got in and buckled up. "Go!"

"What did they want?" she asked, the car in idle.

I pointed to Velma and Zelma, their offspring trailing behind the women as they charged at us. "We need to leave. Now!"

Seeing this would not end well, Pearlie jammed the gas to the floor and left Ron's angry family in our dusty wake.

On the way back to the office, I explained our predicament. Even with Ron's contract drawn up by an attorney, the two sisters could tie us up in court, making it impossible to get our licenses, much less stay in business.

Pearlie huffed out a sigh and swung into the nearest McDonald's. "As scary as those two are, we gotta come up with a plan. Let's get something to eat."

My stomach churned. The thought of eating made me nauseous, but not Pearlie. I got out and followed her inside.

I was given the job of filling up our drinks, while she carried the heavily laden tray of a double cheeseburger and large fries to a table.

"What we need," she said popping a fry into her mouth, "is a way to distract those two so we can get back to solving these cases, collect our payment from Damian's mother and get our license."

"Good luck with that," I said, my voice wobbling with frustration. "They'll take us to court. This could drag out for years. We'll lose everything we've worked for."

She took a bite out of the burger, swallowed and took a gulp of her drink. "You got me *diet* Coke? Did you know that Aspertame forces your body to think you're using a lot more sugar and that it actually makes you more hungry than if you'd just had regular sugar?"

"No, the thought never occurred to me—probably because all I can think of is what I'm going to do for a living and flipping burgers is not on that tiny list!"

"Keep your voice down, will ya?" Pearlie picked the onion out of her burger. "I told them no onions. What was I trying to say before you gave me that poisonous diet drink? Oh yeah, what can we give those two that will make them back off?"

I took in a deep breath and blew it out, trying to calm my mounting panic. "That last twenty grand we owed Ron, but don't have?"

"And what do *we* want?" she asked, taking the last bite of her burger.

"Money to pay our bills?"

"Oh, come on. You're so wound up, you're not hearing yourself," she said, wiping her lips of the last of her burger. "Have some fries."

I pulled a fry out of the bag and chewed. It might as well have been sand in my mouth. "There's nothing wrong with my hearing. We're screwed five ways to Sunday and it's all Ron's fault."

Pearlie sighed. "Of course it's his fault, but there's nothing we can do about it now."

"We don't have the twenty grand to pay them and it's too late to kill Ron for all the crap he's put us through."

Pearlie put another French fry in her mouth and chewed. "Did you know that they both got laid off from their jobs?"

"Fascinating. At least they'll get unemployment. We get nothing."

"Right. But back to what I was sayin'. What if we offer to pay Zelma and Velma the last of what we owed Ron, but they have to work it off by helping at the office?"

"You're the super financial wiz in the family, so where do we get the money to pay for secretaries?" I was beginning to sound a bit squeaky.

"They've got unemployment, don't they? We got two cases to solve. They can answer phones while keeping an eye on us. If nothing else, they'll see for themselves that we're not withholding anything from them."

I felt my stomach turn over. "You really think it'll work?"

"Might as well ask them," she said, nodding at the two women and four teenagers coming through the door.

"Oh crap! They followed us?"

147

"Everybody's gotta eat," Pearlie said, waving the sisters over.

So do rattlesnakes and poisonous spiders, but that doesn't mean we have to be on the menu.

The two accepted Pearlie's invitation to join us. Burgers all around seemed to calm the suspicious sisters and settle their offspring long enough for Pearlie to outline her plan.

After firing off questions, they looked at each other, nodded and stuck out their hands.

"You want a contract?" Pearlie asked.

Zelma cracked a grin. "What for? The sooner we solve these cases, the sooner you can pay us."

"We'll take the kids home and meet you at your office," Velma said.

An hour later, they joined us in the office where we showed them our evidence board.

I was impressed when the sisters whipped out identical notebooks and jotted the particulars of each case.

"Even if Wade did kill Ron, we still have the cold case to solve on Damian's father."

"What time tomorrow?" Velma asked.

"Do we get a key to the office?" Zelma asked.

"We don't want to be seen standing around in the hallway," Velma said.

"We'd look like criminals trying to break in," Zelma finished.

"And where do we sit?" Velma asked, looking around the office space.

"Use Ron's desk, or ours, when we're not here," I said.

The sisters gave Ron's desk a baleful look and I took pity on them. "I'll pick up folding tables and chairs tonight and you girls can fight over who gets what tomorrow."

Pearlie reached into her handbag and handed Zelma her key. "Nine a.m. is fine, and I'll get another one made tomorrow."

Satisfied with the arrangements, they left.

"They'll have gone through everything in this office by the time we get here tomorrow," I said, wearily.

"I sure hope so. Maybe they'll come up with some more business."

She was right, of course. While our file cabinets held nothing but closed cases, the sisters might yet be able to squeeze some new business out of those old files.

"What're you going to do for a key?" I asked.

Pearlie, well aware that I was unable to break my early morning habit as an aero-ag pilot, said, "Someone will be here at nine a.m. It just won't be me."

"It's already five-thirty. I'd like to think that I could go home and enjoy a nice dinner with my husband but I'd rather not tell Caleb I'm looking into a rumor about his best friend. I think I should make that call and see if I can drive up there now."

"Sooner the better," Pearlie said, flipping through the newspaper.

"Do you have any plans for tonight?"

"Like you said, any other day I'd be having dinner," she said, opening a drawer and smacking a file folder onto the desk, "but tonight I'll be here going over the old photos of the shoot-out. Call me if the woman has anything concrete on Andy Sokolov."

I had my doubts. Why had she kept quiet all these years? Had someone interviewed the daughter and decided the girl had lied? Hormonal teenagers had been known to tell tales for the attention. Or had she been paid off?

I left a message for Caleb telling him I was working late, then left for the hour-and-a-half drive to Tucson thinking if she wasn't at home or had changed her mind about seeing me, I'd stop by Costco and pick up supplies for the office and home.

I enjoyed my solo drive listening to National Public Radio instead of country western music, but at the Kolb exit, I hit the Blue Tooth and dialed Margaret Painter's number. She answered the phone as if she'd been sitting on it.

Her home was a single story ranch house south of the University of Arizona and I no sooner put a foot out of the car than she was at the door, waiting. She was calmly observing me, as I was her. I got out, closed the car door and waved.

She waved back.

As I got to the porch, she looked up and smiled. "It's still hot out here," she said, backing her wheelchair up to make room for me to come inside.

Someone forgot to tell me Andy Sokolov's accuser was in a wheelchair.

Chapter Eighteen:

Margaret Painter wheeled her chair aside and I slipped into the cool house while she closed the front door. "Some years I keep the A/C on almost to Thanksgiving. Can I offer you some iced tea or a soda?"

"Water would be great," I said.

"Have a seat in the living room and I'll bring it out."

I thanked her and stepped into her living room. The house looked to be tiled throughout, the grout worn in a few places, making me think the house had been tiled some years back.

There was no clutter to trip a wheelchair and the furniture was simple and spare. The dining room had an oak dining table with dusty and never used place mats, a sofa against the window, the soft indentation in one corner and a TV tray on wheels pushed to the side. Pictures in frames on the walls appeared to be the only decoration. All of them of her and a child who progressed in age until the last one where she looked to be about fifteen.

"One water for you and a Sprite for me," she said, setting the tray on the coffee table and handing me the cold glass of water with ice. "They grow up so fast. Do you have children, Ms Bains?"

Unable to think of a suitable reason other than my own personal tardiness, I simply said, "No, I'm sorry to say, I haven't."

I stood where I was, waiting to see if she would transfer to the sofa or if she wanted me to stay long enough to be seated.

She motioned me to the sofa and picked up her glass. "You're not with social services?"

"No, I'm a private investigator."

"How much were you told about my allegations against Andy Sokolov?"

"Not much. We have another case, totally unrelated, but his name came up and I'd like to hear your side."

"You won't be able to do anything with it. He'll deny it all. He's very good at denial. A real charmer our Andy."

I brought out my notebook a little powder pink mini-recorder. It looks just enough like toy to appear non-threatening.

Holding it in my hands, I said, "Would you mind if I recorded our conversation? I can take notes, but my handwriting is so bad, sometimes even I can't read it."

She stared at the recorder for a minute. "It's just for your notes, right? What I tell you won't get back to him, will it?"

I put the notebook and recorder on the table and leaned back into the cushions. "That depends. What would you like to see happen to Andy Sokolov?"

Her face scrunched into a mask of pain. "I'd love to see him go to prison for what he did to us."

"I thought you might say that," I said, picking up the recorder. I turned it on and laid it on the coffee table. When we finished the preliminaries, I asked her to tell me her side of the story.

"I've been sober for fourteen years, eight months and twenty days. That's almost fifteen years to the day since he molested my daughter." She paused, taking another sip of her drink before continuing.

"I deeply regret the years I was lost in self-pity and alcohol. AA taught me that nothing but sobriety would give me a chance at life again.

"My husband left when Bonnie was five. We were both drinkers then. Fighters too, not all of it his fault, some of it was mine, but it took a toll. Drinking leads to spiteful, hurtful words, and then someone cheats on someone and it all ends in divorce court. He paid child support, but I gave him such a bad time about the money, that after a while he just stopped with the visits, the phone calls and the child-support. I tried the courts but a man can go off the grid and just vanish, you know."

In a voice filled with self-loathing, she continued. "I didn't care. I had a job. I had my work, my kid and my booze. In case you've never heard the term, that's called a functioning alcoholic. Two steps one way or the other and I would've been a falling down drunk. And if I hadn't had Bonnie, I'm sure I would've been found dead in a gutter. Yet, for all my self-pity, my self-serving grandiose opinion of myself, I had no idea my poor baby would think it was her fault that her daddy wasn't here. We never really know what little kids think. I sure never thought to ask her. Too busy.

"When Bonnie turned fifteen, she decided it was my fault that her daddy never came around, or sent birthday or Christmas gifts. I knew having a teenager is like doing hard time. She was already difficult, all over the place with black lipstick and seventeen-year-old boyfriends. I was at my wit's end. Then Andy showed up and asked if Bonnie would like to join his softball team, I was elated. Softball? Yeah sure, why not?"

"How did you find out?" I asked.

"She started coming home late from practice. I would have dinner waiting and her excuse was that she and Andy's family went to pizza or she had to wait for him to finish a meeting with the other coaches. I think it was about the third time she waltzed in at nine o'clock on a school night and I told her I'd have to talk to Andy about these late nights. I remember thinking how I would regret not having his help if he dropped her. I was thinking of me. Not my daughter.

"But then she looked at the half-empty glass in my hand and lifted her chin in that way she would do when she was feeling defiant and she said, 'You're not ever going to take me away from Andy. Not like you did with Daddy. Andy won't allow it.'

"I put down my drink, got out of my chair and slapped her across the face. Wasn't that what a mother is supposed to do when her fifteen-year-old daughter smarts off to her? But I wasn't listening, was I? Not with two-fifths of vodka swimming through my veins. But I thought about those words all the next day at work and when I came home, there was a note on the kitchen table that said Andy had picked her up for practice. I called his wife. No practice to-night, his wife said. I was too proud and too scared to say the words, what I suspected, so I went looking on my own. My last option was the backside of the Lavender Pit mine. You know that place where the kids go to park? He had a '57 Chevy he'd remodeled and the damn thing was rocking. The bastard. I flew out of my car, ran to the passenger side and yanked her out of that car so fast she didn't have time to cover herself. I was a mad woman, screaming profanities at them both, telling him I was going to ruin him as I shoved her toward our car.

"Bonnie was crying and buttoning her dress when I started the down-hill drive and home. I told her to buckle up, but I don't think she heard me, or maybe it was just another way to defy me. It was her last," she said, unable to finish, she swiped at the tears running down her cheeks.

"Then what happened?" I asked.

"He came after us. I felt the bumper nudge up on mine. He backed off, flashing his lights. He wanted me to stop. He wanted to talk. Bonnie laughed and waved at him. 'Pull over,' she said. Like it was all some crazy game that I refused to play.

"When I wouldn't pull over, he continued to follow us down the hill. By this time, Bonnie and I were yelling at each other, me accusing, her blaming. She swore at me and grabbed at the wheel. He must've seen us struggling and this time his nudge caught a corner, shoving the car into the side of the mountain. Naturally, I yanked the wheel back the other way and before I knew it, we were going off the road and over the cliff. Over and over and over. Three hundred feet they said, to the bottom."

"The wheelchair—is it the result of your accident?"

"Or you can call it my just desserts," she said reaching over and picking up a music box in the shape of a boat with a sailor boy in it. "I was legally drunk."

"And Bonnie?" I asked quietly.

"That picture of her on the wall? That was her sophomore prom. It's the last picture I have of her. I was convicted of negligent manslaughter, got probation and court ordered rehab. Andy got off scot free. So what do you think, Ms. Bains? Any ideas on how you can nail Mayor Sokolov for having sex with a fifteen-year-old?"

I shook my head. "Do you know if there were other girls he might've molested?"

She put the music box on the table. "I haven't kept in touch with anyone in Wishbone. Not for the last ten or so years. I have a job at the library in Tucson and I attend AA, but child molesters are never really rehabilitated, are they?"

"I wish I knew the answer," I said, and stood. "But I'll certainly see what I can do. I have a long drive home. Could I use your bathroom before I go?"

"Sure," she said, "there's only the one and it's at the end of the hallway."

I used the sound of the flushing toilet to open her medicine cabinet. Bottles lined up like little soldiers ready to battle viruses and bacteria of the wheelchair bound. The one I was looking for was also there; oxycodone, a strong painkiller favored by addicts. Looking at the date, the quantity in the prescription and the number of tablets left in the bottle, I was relieved to see that she hadn't exchanged one addiction for another.

When I came back into the living room, she was winding up the music box. "He came to the hospital while they were still working to save my spine. He brought flowers and this music box and told me how it was all going to play out. He'd retained a lawyer and he'd do everything he could to see that I got probation, but it wouldn't do me or my case any good to accuse him of sexual abuse, not when everyone knew I was an unreliable mother and a drunk. Then he put the music box on the over-bed table where it was out of my reach and flipped the switch. I had to lay there in traction, tears streaming down my face while the music box played, *My Bonnie Lies Over the Ocean*. You know that song? I keep it to remind myself," she said, releasing the switch and letting a verse tinkle out before turning it off. "That's the kind of man Andy Sokolov is."

She opened the front door and once again wheeled aside to allow me to leave. I turned to her and held out my hand. She took it and looked up at me, the question in her sad eyes.

"You understand," I said, "I can't guarantee anything."

"Bringing Andy Sokolov to justice would take a miracle, but I can hope, can't I?"

I should regret leaving her with any kind of hope. A miracle would be a long shot, yet, I would never again hear that children's song without thinking of Andy Sokolov's cruelty. If it took me a lifetime, I would find a way to make that miracle happen.

Now I had to take this sad tale home to my husband. Would I be able to convince him that his friendship with Andy Sokolov was tragically wasted?

Chapter Nineteen:

By the time I got home, I felt as if my brain had been lacquered in black from the ugliness that happens when adults force their twisted desires on helpless children. Yes, I've heard plenty of stories of abuse against women, but as I would never put up with abuse from anyone, I was always able to draw a line between them and me. Children were another subject, and I felt out of my element, unable to do anything but listen. The bad feeling didn't dissipate when I let myself in and dropped my keys on the small table by the door.

There was a ball game on in the living room. I heard the refrigerator door open and glass bottles clinking together. I walked into the kitchen and Caleb saluted me with two bottles.

"Hi sweetheart. Want one? Your dad and I are watching the game."

"Sure," I said. "Let me wash up and I'll join you."

Reprieved for at least the three minutes it took to run a washcloth over my face and draw a brush through my hair, I went into the living room, accepted the beer and asked Caleb to put the game on hold. "I have some news."

Caleb turned from the still image on the TV screen to look for signs that I'd been in a fight. Seeing I didn't have a black eye, he asked, "What is it? Should you be telling this to Homicide instead of me and your dad?"

"It doesn't directly affect anything we're working on now, but it does involve Andy Sokolov." My father and I exchanged looks. I didn't have to tell him that his prediction about old friends had come true. I told them everything I'd learned from Andy's accuser.

As the story unfolded, Caleb's brows dipped, his mouth tightened and once or twice he'd ask a question or make a comment, usually with an expletive attached. "I've arrested my share of pedophiles and I know that they're never, ever cured and they don't stop unless they're caught and put in prison. He may have gone underground with this, but he hasn't quit. Oh, jeez, he's got a thirty-year-old married son with two little girls. Something has to be done."

"You *do* see that this puts Andy back on Ian's list of suspects?" I asked.

Caleb's head moved back and forth as if to shake off a bad smell. "Ian knew this and didn't tell me."

"Nobody would call Ian Tom a fool," I said. "He handed it off to Pearlie and me hoping we'd ferret out the truth. If it went balls up, it's not on his watch."

"I get it," Caleb said. "I don't like it, but I get it. Andy's dirty little secret needed uncovering, but I'm annoyed that Ian thought he should dump this on you and Pearlie so he can keep his hands clean. The question is—how to prove it?"

"What makes you think that girl was the only one?" Dad said. "He's still coaching, isn't he? Lots of them young girls raised by single moms."

"I dunno Dad," I said. "Parents are more aware of this kind of abuse these days."

Caleb growled, "He didn't get to his position as the mayor of Wishbone by being stupid!"

"You don't have to yell, Caleb."

"Sorry," Caleb said, scrubbing at the top of his buzz cut. "Tomorrow, I'm going to talk to someone I know in Sacramento. He's a criminologist and a profiler. He may be able to put us onto the right track. You and Pearlie have my permission to look as hard as you like at Andy."

He went to the door. "I'm going for a walk."

"It's dark out there," I called after him. "Take a flashlight. Better yet, take Hoover, he could use the exercise."

He clipped on Hoover's leash, picked up a flashlight and without a backward glance, went outside.

I knew this was going to be hard, but I was also grateful that Caleb didn't question the woman's story.

"He'll be all right," my dad said.

"I know. It's just that men like you and Caleb hold your friends to such high standards, that when your trust has been abused you take it very hard."

"It's like a punch to the gut," my dad said, getting off the couch. "The monsoons are supposed to kick in tonight. I better get going before there's a gully washer I can't cross."

Until monsoon season kicks in, summers are hot and dry, but July through August it rains almost every afternoon and sometimes into the night. The rain moves across the desert in cells, drenching one area and leaving whole swaths of dry spots until the next day.

I followed him out the door. Lightning flickered across the southern sky, the smell of rain in the air. "You're not sorry you told me about Andy's accuser, are you?"

"Oh, Lord no. I figured you'd get to the truth of it, one way or the other."

I pecked him on the cheek. "If you see Caleb, tell him to come home before he gets wet."

I was brushing my teeth when the front door slammed shut against the wind and Hoover's collar rattled as he shook water from his coat. Caleb came into the bathroom. "Have we got an old towel? Hoover's soaked and his feet are muddy. "

"Here," I said, tossing him one out of the hamper. "Take him out on the back patio and hose off his feet. Just put the towel in the laundry and I'll wash it tomorrow. And you look chilled; take a hot shower before you come to bed."

I was still tense from our earlier conversation, and knowing Caleb was prone to insomnia if a case was weighing on his mind, I didn't wait up. Still, I fought my way into sleep shoving away the depressing thought that even if Andy wasn't guilty of murdering Damian's father, I would have to find a way to get him on sexual abuse.

Around two a.m., I felt Caleb's weight on the bed as he moved under the sheet, his warm body still damp from a late shower as he pulled me up against him. I reached back and touched his neck where the hair was still wet.

"You were supposed to use a towel," I said.

"I did. Hoover and I shared it."

"You didn't."

"Does it matter, really?"

"In the grand scheme of things, I suppose not."

"I have a plan."

I rolled over to rest my head on his cupped hand. "You do? What is it?"

"The plan is to kiss my wife goodnight and not think about anything else."

"Good one, Caleb Stone."

Chapter Twenty:

"I've been going over the old photos of the shoot-out," Pearlie said, "and I think I've found something."

I came over to her side of the desk and looked through the magnifying glass she kept on a stand. "See this bicycle here at the edge of the photo?"

"Yes, I see it now. A kid's hand on the handlebars and his leg on the ground next to a bike," I said. "He's behind the barricade, but he's also right next to the action. It's a wonder he didn't get shot. He must've been a local kid from around Palominas. I wonder if the sheriff's department ever interviewed him?"

"He's not on the list of witnesses, but I found a news story in the archives about a hit and run on a kid riding his bike down Highway 92. This has to be the same kid. He's about the right age to be riding his bike and he lived in Pal- ominas. No obituary for a twelve-year-old Harley Aldrich. I don't know why they didn't interview him, but if he's still around, he might remember the incident, maybe even ID the shooter."

"Get your laptop open. We'll both look for him, or a parent."

Five minutes later, I said, "A Mavis Aldrich owns a small grocery store in Palominas. That's a location that would be close enough for a curious boy."

With high hopes that we'd just uncovered a witness that the police forgot, we hurried out the door for a chat with the mother.

~~~~~~~~~~~~

Shiny green zucchini, fat tomatoes, yellow squash and herbs of all kinds filled baskets along one wall of the small grocery store.

The girl behind the counter said that Mavis Aldrich was in her garden. "You can't miss it," she said. "Drive east toward Wishbone and turn right at the sign on the highway for her vegetable farm, *Aldrich's Garden of Eaten'*."

Seeing the Jeep drive up her gravel road, a grey-haired woman removed her gardening gloves and waited.

When we explained why we wanted to know about her son, Harley, she invited us inside for a cool glass of water.

"Sure, he was there," she said, looking with interest at Pearlie and me. "All the boys followed the fire trucks. Didn't matter if it was day or night, if they heard sirens they were on their bikes. I used to think it was safe for a kid to ride his bike on Highway 92, that is until someone plowed into my boy and kept going. Hit and run, the police called it and they never found the driver."

"Did anyone from the sheriff's office ever interview your son?"

"No. They didn't, but then he was in the hospital for a week. After that, he had therapy and that kept us busy, but come to think of it, no one ever asked, not even after he came home."

Pearlie and I looked at each other. "Perhaps the accident affected his memory of that day?"

"Oh no," Mavis said with a laugh. "Harley remembers that day like it was yesterday. Let me write down his address. He has a darling little cottage above Wishbone. Now, don't you be put off by his eccentric notions, he's fine where it counts and you'll see, he remembers every detail of that day."

Before we left, Mavis loaded us up with tomatoes, onions and squash as well as her handwritten instructions on how to find Harley's place.

~~~~~~~~~~

Harley Aldrich's cottage was just one of hundreds of cabins built for miners and their families during the heyday of the copper mining in Wishbone. Later, they were renovated and remodeled by artists and visitors who were only too happy to rediscover Wishbone's five-thousand foot elevation and cooler Arizona summers.

Because of the dry climate, the successive layers of paint on Harley's cottage had peeled back here and there so that the house appeared to be having its own psychedelic experiment. There was a garden, a miniature of his mother's, but still well-tended and weed free, and a climbing yellow rose grew over the trellis by the door, added color, fragrance and shade for the entrance.

Before we could knock, the door swung open and a man, his stocky, muscled body filling out a plaid shirt and faded jeans, smiled a welcome. His teeth were remarkably white against a thick black beard. His hair needed a trim, but it was clean and curled behind well-formed ears.

I thought Harley Aldrich might be very good looking if he shaved off the bush hiding his face.

Clear, bright blue eyes inspected us in turn. "Hello, ladies. Mom forgot to give me descriptions, so which one of you is Lalla and which one is Pearlie?"

I stuck out my hand and he shook it. "I'm Lalla Bains," I said, "and this is my cousin, Pearlie Bains."

When Pearlie offered him her hand, Harley took it between his and sighed. "Gosh, you smell good."

Pearlie gaped at the unexpected compliment, but before she could say anything, Harley pointed us to an ancient, lumpy sofa with a hound dog lying across it.

"Beans! Get off. Sorry, I can't seem to break his attachment to that couch," he said, sweeping the dog off the couch. "Oh, wait, I have cookies."

He came back with a plate of cookies and put them on top of the assorted magazines covering the coffee table. "I made these fresh this morning, so dig in."

Harley waited for us to pick a cookie, then snapped his fingers and dashed for the small kitchen. "I forgot milk," he said, his head dipping into the fridge.

Pearlie frowned and mouthed, "What's wrong with him?"

Unwilling to say anything that might embarrass our host, I elbowed her to keep quiet.

Pearlie muttered at the insult and struggled out of the saggy couch to inspect the wall of colorful photos with sticky notes next to them. She turned to me and thumbed over her shoulder the silent question on her lips, *What's this?*

I cautioned her to keep quiet with a finger to my lips, but I knew we were both beginning to wonder if we'd stumbled onto some kind of stalker.

He came back into the room with two glasses of milk.

"Gotta have milk with cookies," he said, thrusting the glasses into our hands.

Pearlie nodded. "What's with the photos of people?"

He looked over to the wall. "People? Oh that. I ask for permission, but most folks don't mind. It helps me remember them for next time. I hope you'll let me take your picture before you leave. Especially you, Pearlie. I wouldn't want to forget you."

My earlier excitement at a new lead just plummeted. "Do you mind telling us about that, Harley?"

"Oh sure, I don't mind. It was the accident that did it, or so I'm told. I don't remember much of it. I recognized everyone in my family, but every time the doctor walked into the room, he was a stranger all over again. At first I was terrified and then embarrassed until the doc explained that it might or might not be permanent. I worked with a therapist and learned to compensate for the damage with a keen sense of smell. So you see, I'll remember you, Pearlie, even without that nice perfume of yours," he said, his eyes unabashedly admiring my cousin. "Everyone says I'm getting better at remembering new people when I meet them, but just in case, I keep names attached to the photos. Outside of that little problem, I can do everything a regular guy can do."

Pearlie's eyes pleaded for help.

"Your mother said you could tell us about the shooting?" I asked.

"Oh sure. Like it was yesterday," he said with a laugh. "My therapist said it's because that was the last time my brain worked on all cylinders. Did my mom tell you how much I used to love chasing fire engines?"

"Yes, she did and she told us how she knew she couldn't stop you even if she wanted to."

Harley beamed. "That's me… well, it used to be. I'm not twelve years old anymore, but I can still hear the squeal of the fire engine tires and smell the smoke."

"So you rode your bike to where the sheriff's deputies and the church people were shooting at each other?" I asked.

"They weren't shooting when I got there, but the church people had set a wooden barricade on fire to keep everyone out and they were throwing rocks and shouting at the deputies. Then someone brought out rifles and I could see that the deputies were scared and didn't know what to do. I suppose it's not a nice thing to say, but I remember thinking the place seemed to reek of fire and hate. I'm sorry, Pearlie, did I upset you?"

"No, no," she said. "I-I was… thinking of… uh, something else. Go on. What did you see next?"

"One of the church members was shot that day," I said. "Did you see it happen?"

Harley's lips rolled in until they disappeared into his thick beard. "Well as they say in the old westerns, 'that was a dirty, low down thing to do, shooting a man in the back.'"

Though several people were shot that day, including one of the deputies, the only person shot in the back was Damian's father. "Yes, it was. Then did you see who shot him?"

He looked up at me with surprise. "Sure I did."

Relieved that our trip was not a waste of time, I took out the black and white photos I'd brought with us. "Could you look at these photos and let us know if you see him?"

Harley nodded and said, "I can try."

Seeing there wasn't a flat surface on the coffee table, he swept the magazines onto the floor. "I'll pick them up later. Let's see what you have."

I spread out photos of the crime scene.

He squatted on his muscular haunches to examine each picture, and in turn named the locals from Palominas, the deputies he knew from the time he was in grade school, and finally the partial image of a twelve-year-old Harley next to his bike. "Hey, I didn't know anyone had taken a picture of me that day."

"Well?" Pearlie asked, her voice an impatient growl. "Do you or don't you see him?"

At her sharp tone, a puzzled expression appeared in his eyes. "Not in these, I don't. Do you have any more?"

"No, sorry. That's all we have," I said, putting the pictures back into my file and standing up to leave.

Harley backed away, brushing at imaginary dust on his pant legs. Pearlie's impatience had struck a nerve and he used the gesture to symbolically brush away the episode as if it never happened.

When he looked up, I could see the intelligence that most people, myself included, probably missed. Harley had a glitch with something we all take for granted, but he wasn't an idiot and he was still a man who liked to look at a pretty girl.

"We'd better be going," Pearlie said, sidling for the door.

Harley rushed to grab his camera. "Please wait. I need to take your picture... for next time."

I smiled while he aimed his camera at me, but at the click of the lens, the door slammed shut. Pearlie had fled without saying goodbye, much less saying thanks for the cookies.

I apologized for my cousin, but Harley just laughed and rubbed a hand across his beard. "It's the beard. Scares little children, dogs and pretty girls. Maybe I'll shave it, but just between you and me, I won't have any problem remembering her, even without the photo."

At the Jeep, I got in and buckled up. "Well, that was incredibly rude."

"Why?" she asked. "We were here to see if he could ID a killer, not hang out with a guy who takes pictures of people he won't remember tomorrow."

I stared at my cousin. She had deliberately trampled on this nice man's feelings, but it would do no good to bring that up now. "Have you completely forgotten the rule for interviewing witnesses? We're supposed to make nice, empathize, create a bond, and generally do anything we can to get them talking."

"I got empathy in spades and making nice isn't going to help us one little bit. No wonder no one bothered to interview him. His testimony wouldn't stand up in court."

I fumbled to find an appropriate response. She was right of course, but right now, I just wanted to wring her neck.

I wondered if Harley would put up my picture, better yet, would he even bother to record his meeting with my heart breaker cousin?

Chapter Twenty-one:

Leaving Harley's house, I took the roundabout for home, then on a whim, pulled into Wishbone's police station. I closed the car door on Pearlie's objections and walked to the entrance. At times like this, I could not understand why she would be rude to someone like Harley Aldrich, so I didn't care what she thought of the impromptu stop. She could sulk in the car.

I leaned on the counter and knocked on the heavy glass partition. "Hey Betty. Is he in?"

She smiled and buzzed the door open.

He was reading a file, his feet up on his desk, leaning back in his dad's old wooden office chair, the one thing he'd insisted on bringing from California to his new job as police chief of Wishbone, Arizona.

He let his feet drop off the desk. "What're you doing in town?"

"We went to interview Harley Aldrich. You know him?"

"Harley? Yeah, sure. He cuts and delivers oak wood to folks who still have fireplaces. Why Harley?"

"Damian, of course. That's the one case that still has money on the table."

He held up a finger. "Uh, about Harley...."

"Yeah, we know. His mother wasn't exactly forthcoming on that issue, but I suppose if we had thought to ask anyone in law enforcement they would've told us his testimony wouldn't fly in court."

Relieved to see that I wasn't going to argue for putting Harley on the stand, he said, "Harley's okay. You saw him last Friday night. He plays fiddle with a blue grass band at Screaming Banshee Pizza. "

I tried to remember Harley in the band of five guys. All those bushy beards looked the same to me. I lifted my shoulders to show my complete ignorance.

"He wears an old floppy gray fedora with the brim turned down," Caleb said, "and ancient coveralls. It's all part of their look—Wishbone's version of the Soggy Bottom Boys."

"Oh, now I remember. He was great on the violin, but how does he get along? I mean without remembering the people he meets?"

"He recognizes everyone he knew from before the accident and luckily that's most of the residents in Wishbone," Caleb said. "And I hear he compensates with a keen sense of smell."

"Not very romantic, but he certainly seemed to like the way Pearlie smelled," I said.

I wouldn't bring up Pearlie's terse reaction to Harley. Caleb still had doubts about Pearlie as my business partner. Hot headed he'd called her. But then that's what people used to say about me, too.

"Have they found Wade Hamilton yet?" I asked. "Or his body?"

"Not yet," he said, picking up a thick file, "But the sheriff's department has Emily's and Joey Green's statements and the DA is ready to charge him with grand theft auto—that is if he shows up alive. Right now, I'm reading up on local copper thieves. A whole family of them, if you can believe that."

"That's sad."

"It's like being in the Ozarks, hunting bootleggers."

"Are you hearing banjo music?" At his bewildered expression, I said, "Never mind. How *does* one steal copper?"

"This family will steal any metal they can get their hands on, but when the price of copper is up, they go for the wires and pipes out of vacant homes and businesses. We got a call this morning after someone spotted one of the brothers running away from an open manhole. There were two of them, one as look-out and the other to go down a manhole and cut out the copper wire."

"They didn't know the wires were hot?"

"If they were smarter they'd be doing something else, now wouldn't they? And the idiot left his dead brother for us to find."

"It's getting late," I said, looking at my watch, "and Pearlie is waiting in the car. So dinner out or should we go home and eat?"

"Let's eat out. I'll meet you in the parking lot."

There was a note under the windshield of my Jeep. *I got a ride to Screaming Banshee's Pizza. I'll save you and Caleb a seat or I can get a ride home.*

I held out the note to Caleb. "I guess we're eating at Screaming Banshee's."

By the time we got to the pizza place all of the outdoor tables were full and the musicians were tuning their instruments.

"Over here!" Pearlie waved at us from a table by the wall.

"You know the guys playing tonight?" I asked.

She giggled. "I know the one tuning his fiddle." She pointed at Harley, his ear to the *f* hole on his violin. He saw us and waved.

"Harley doesn't seem to have a problem remembering us," I said.

Pearlie's smile was tenuous. "He may not remember our faces, but I gotta hand it to him, he sure knows how to live for today."

I wasn't about to sully her good mood by reminding her of her earlier bad manners toward Harley. "How'd you end up here?" I asked.

She looked down at her hands, an embarrassed blush staining her cheeks. "I was hot, tired and hungry, so I thought I'd hitch a ride into Wishbone, get something to eat. Then Harley and his pals drove up, pulled me into their truck and here I am."

I looked over at Harley and his band members. Maybe Harley's *carpe diem* was rubbing off on my cousin.

Nik arrived with two large pizzas. "Hey, guys. Harley ordered two kinds, so I hope you're hungry."

She laid the pizzas on the table and returned with a pitcher each of root beer and beer on tap.

"I figure if someone else is driving, I might as well enjoy myself," she said, reaching for the beer.

I ignored the implication that she would be going home with one of the band members and poured root beer for Caleb and me.

"And let's not talk about murder tonight, okay?" she said. "I've had enough sad stories for one day. Let's just eat and listen to some music."

What was it about Harley that brought out the worst and then the best in my cousin?

By the time the pizza, drinks and the last set was finished, Caleb rose to pay the bill, but Nik waved away his money. "Harley took care of it. You staying for the encore, Pearlie?"

"Shuuure." Pearlie, I noticed, had single-handedly finished the pitcher of beer.

Nik winked at us and said, "One of us will see she gets home all right."

I looked from Nik to the band wondering whose home she meant.

Caleb leaned on the Jeep. "Looks like it's going to rain. Tomorrow I have to take the Garza boys up to the res. You want to go with me?"

An entire day spent with my husband sounded good. Besides, we could use the time to discuss the case. "Sounds good to me. I'll see you at home."

I drove home under clouds chasing each other across a starlit sky. The wonder of Arizona was that when the rain stopped, the air cleared so that constellations seemed to spread from horizon to horizon. If it wasn't raining by the time we were ready for bed, we'd take our sleeping bags and go up on the flat roof of our house and watch the sky until we fell asleep. That made me very happy. Or was it the fun music, or the idea that I wouldn't have to contend with a hungover business partner tomorrow morning?

Chapter Twenty-two:

We never made it up to the roof last night, as rain hit the minute we got home. But sleeping inside only got me another strange dream. This time I'm in a submarine in the bottom of a lake. Naturally it's a yellow submarine, but at least there's Beatle's music to go along with it. A hand reaches down, grabs the submarine and pulls us out of the water. Dumb dreams.

I rolled over and nudged Caleb. "You starting coffee or am I?"

"It's Saturday," he mumbled into his pillow. "Officially my day off, right?"

"Oh yeah," I said, blinking my way out of sleep. "Except we have to take the Garza brothers to the res today." I slapped his butt. "Get up and get in the shower. I'll make the coffee."

I dropped my feet over the edge of the bed and slipped into a pair of flip flops. Since it was monsoon season, none of us went barefoot in the house for fear of stepping on a scorpion. These small, light on their feet critters seemed to dislike getting rained on as much as the next person and scurried for cover with every downpour. Unfortunately, they didn't always scurry fast enough, and retaliation was a wickedly painful sting from the end of an upright tail.

The kitchen wall clock we'd brought from Dad's home in California said six a.m. We'd pick up the Garza brothers at eight a.m., head up to the Chiricahua Apache reservation and get them to the foster parents who had signed on to feed and board them until their mother would be released from rehab.

Coffee started, I heard Caleb get in the shower. I was tempted to join him, but our time this morning would have to be by the clock. The matron at Juvie expected us to be on time.

I dressed, left Caleb's cup on the counter and a note that I'd taken Hoover over to my dad's.

~~~~~~~~~~

Hearing voices coming from the back of the house, I cinched Hoover onto a leash and led him around to the back patio.

I was surprised to see Coco Lucero in a frilly apron over white slacks and cotton shirt, a tray with coffee pot and mugs in her hands. She was all smiles until she saw Hoover, then her eyes went wide and the tray wobbled precariously.

My dad sprang out of his chair to catch the tray before it slipped out of her hands. "It's only Hoover," he said. "Don't worry, he's friendly."

Hoover, totally unconcerned with the idea that his reputation might be maligned, flopped down next to my dad.

Though I knew he was only doing it to calm Coco, Dad reached over and accepted the dog's leash.

"Buenos días, Señora," she said, keeping an eye on the dog. "Will you join us for coffee?"

"Thanks, but I just brought Hoover home." I smiled down affectionately at Hoover. Completely relaxed; tongue lolling in a wide doggie grin, Hoover was perfectly happy to lie here for the rest of the year.

"He live *here*?" she said, her delicate brows drawn together in dismay.

Seeing that we were not going to contradict her, she scooted her chair another couple of inches away.

Generally, Hoover had the run of the house, the yard and went everywhere with my dad. He was not only good company, but ever since the mine collapse, he was also Dad's bodyguard.

"Caleb and I have to take the Garza brothers to the Chiricahua Reservation today and it's a long drive. We don't want to leave Hoover alone in the house all day."

"He can stay with us," Dad said.

Us? I looked at him for an explanation, but he ignored my questioning stare and poured a cup of coffee for Coco and then himself. What was this? Was she his housekeeper or his new love interest?

Looking up as if surprised to see that I was still there, he said, "If you go to Costco, could you pick up some things for us?"

There was that *us* again. "Uh, sure. If you have the list ready."

Dad looked at Coco, who took a piece of paper out of her apron pocket and handed it to me. "He is out of everything."

The list was written in a woman's hand. Yep, definitely his housekeeper.

But she was also wearing mascara, lipstick and a distinctive perfume. Maybe she was his girlfriend. But as my daddy would say, *None of your business, Missy.*

I excused myself and left for the short drive home, wondering if it was too late to call our old housekeeper and beg her to come save my dad from the man-eater who'd taken up residence in his home.

~~~~~~~~~~~~~

We picked up the Garza boys at eight a.m., but we only got as far as Benson before they started begging us to stop at McDonalds.

"Didn't they feed you breakfast?" I asked.

"Gruel," the younger boy said with a theatrical sigh. "That's all we've had for days."

"It wasn't gruel, dummy. It was mushy oatmeal and fruit," his brother said. "At home we get McDonald's."

Caleb and I looked at each other. Of course they did. Their mother kept them on a diet of fast food because she had a steady date with a bottle of whiskey. Since this might be the last McDonald's they would get for some time, we swung into the drive-through and got the boys their burger fix, then got back onto the highway.

They unwrapped their meals and polished it all off with milkshakes and fries. When they were finished, they rolled down the window and threw the wrappers out.

"Stop that!" I said, swatting at them over the back of the seat. It was too dangerous to pull over and make them get out and pick it up. Besides, by the time it took for us to stop, the wind would've blown it all into the desert.

I glared at the two miscreants. "There's a fine for littering, you know. Just count yourselves lucky there was no DPS patrolman behind us."

The boys snickered.

If I thought Damian was a pain in the butt, these two made him look like a southern gentleman. "You two behave yourselves."

"Or what?" the older one said. "You'll take us back to Juvie?"

"Yeah," his little brother echoed. "We got a new family waiting for us."

"You don't want to disappoint them, do you?" The older brother's singsong taunt was intended as a dare, but it was easy to see that he was as nervous of the future as his little brother.

I would probably never have children of my own. Good thing too, because I wouldn't want to have ones like these two. Yet, I knew that underneath the bravado, they were just two frightened little boys who were being sent off to live with complete strangers in a new and alien environment.

An hour into the ride, the younger boy started kicking the back seat.

"Stop that," I said. "We're passing farm land. Count cows."

"There's no cows," he said. "You know any jokes?"

"Can't think of any," I said, knowing he was going to tell me one.

"I got a knock-knock joke," he said.

His older brother snickered. "Not that old thing again."

"What do you know, Mom says it's funny."

"When she's drunk everything is funny," the older one muttered.

"Okay, I'll bite," I said. "What's your knock-knock joke?"

Pleased at my willingness to hear his joke, he said, "Knock-knock."

"Who's there?" I answered.

"Orange," he said, with a giggle.

"Orange, who?"

"Orange you glad to see me?"

His little boy enthusiasm was so genuine, so pleased to have a surprise punch line I couldn't help but laugh. I reached over the backrest and tickled his ribs. "That's a good one, now sit back and look for clouds shaped like houses."

Instead, he leaned his chin on the backrest. "You got any kids?"

"No, we don't," I said, glancing at Caleb's profile. His mouth tweaked up in a slight smile. It was my fault, I'd encouraged the kid and now I was his pal.

"Then what do you do all day?" he asked.

"I work."

"Where do you work?"

Thinking of the simplest way to explain what a P.I. does, I said, "I'm an investigator. I find people."

"You do? Could you find my dad?"

His older brother grabbed him by the shirt and pulled him back onto the seat. "Shut up about that, doofus."

"You shut up," his little brother said, his voice quivering. "If we had a dad, we wouldn't be going to live with Indians."

"What's wrong with Indians?" I asked. "You're part Apache."

The little one pulled himself up to the backrest again. "Our step-brother says injuns can't hold their liquor and since Mom's half Indian, we'll end up just like her."

I heard Caleb take a deep breath and let it out, but he still refused to be drawn into the conversation.

"Well," I said. "I think the best way to avoid becoming an alcoholic is to not start drinking in the first place."

"What's a aka-akaholic?"

"An alcoholic is someone who is addicted to alcohol."

That stumped him for a minute and then he said, "Are you an akaholic?"

"No," I said, "But I'm beginning to understand why your mother might be."

"Well, my mom's not an akaholic. She only drinks whiskey."

I punched Caleb for laughing out loud.

Pleased to see that his comment was so well received, the little boy beamed and said, "I know a song. Want me to sing it for you?"

"Sure," I said, reaching over to pat Caleb's arm. "It'll make the trip go quicker."

~~~~~~~~~

We were met at the reservation office by a social worker who accepted the paperwork Caleb handed her.

"Well, are you ready?" she said cheerfully to the boys. "I hear they have horses to ride."

I felt a small, sticky hand take hold of mine, and looking down, a pair of brown eyes telegraphed his fear. I looked at Caleb for help, but figured he had his own problems. The older one was hanging on his sleeve. "What is it?" Caleb asked, frowning down at the boy.

"We'll be good," he said, swallowing hard. "I promise. Please don't leave us here."

The social worker just smiled. "Now, boys, don't make it any harder than it already is. You're going to get a nice home with kids to play with, and don't forget the horses."

I don't know why, but I blurted, "We'll go with you, won't we, Caleb?"

~~~~~~~~~

The mother showed the boys two double beds in the room they would share with the younger children. The little ones were about three and five and they both were using their sleeves to wipe matching drippy noses.

The Garza brothers cast us sorrowful looks. "Do we have to sleep in the same bed? We don't at home."

I had no reply for that, but the social worker said, "You can sleep on the floor if you like, but a double bed is plenty for two, especially if you keep to your own side."

The social worker did ask where the two older boys slept and was assured that the boys were fine in the barn. I gasped. Winter was coming, for crying out loud. Who let their kids sleep in a barn in the winter? Feeling Caleb's restraining hand on my elbow I shut off thoughts of vermin in the straw and two teenagers covered with snow every morning.

The father, seeing the look on my face, deadpanned, "It's warm by our standards, but then we're Apache."

After that, I kept my face a mask of indifference and waited while the social worker inspected the kitchen, checked the source of their water and made sure the safety valve on the propane tank was tight. She ticked things off her list and asked more questions, while the two older boys silently checked us out; our light skin, blond hair, blue eyes, the quality of the boots we wore, Caleb's police uniform, his holstered weapon and the radio on his utility belt.

Caleb noticed the speculative looks too and kept a hand on his sidearm.

When they finished inspecting us, their dark eyes shot arrows at the usurpers. Never mind the little ones with colds, the Garza boys were going to have a hard time fitting in with the teenagers.

The father assured the social worker that he would enroll the boys in the reservation school, see that they got to the bus stop every morning; and pick them up every afternoon. After school, everyone had chores, but there would be time for play and they could ride the horses.

When it was time to say good-bye, the Garza brothers followed us out, hanging on until the social worker gently pulled them away. "I'm sorry," she said. "Goodbyes are never easy, but they're going to do just fine here, you'll see."

Against my better judgment, we left the boys with their foster family; the ones whose two bedroom home was already filled to capacity and whose teenagers didn't look happy about the additional mouths to feed.

~~~~~~~~~~~~~~

Caleb and I argued all the way home. I was a wreck leaving those two children at the reservation but Caleb insisted that I'd been duped by a couple of miniature con artists. Besides, the family had been vetted by social services and they weren't going to mistreat the little buggers. Chances were more than likely to be the other way round. And they only had to stay until their mother got out of rehab, one month at the most. What could possibly go wrong in just a month?

Chapter Twenty-three:

Both of our phones were ringing. Caleb reached for his on the nightstand while I got out of bed to retrieve mine from my purse.

I was a little fuzzy on the uptake, but I didn't have to say much anyway since Pearlie was doing all the talking.

"Pearlie, can you just cut to the chase? We had to go up to the reservation to deliver the Garza brothers to a family and I barely got any sleep last night."

My cousin didn't bother to apologize. "Jesse Jefferson is dead. He was found hung from a church rafter this morning."

I looked over at Caleb. He had his cell between his ear and shoulder, awkwardly zipping up his pants and stepping into his boots.

When he hung up, I asked, "You got the same call?"

"Jesse's church is in Wishbone, so it's my jurisdiction."

"You shave and wash up, I'll start the coffee."

I went back to my conversation with Pearlie. "Caleb just got the call. Where are you?"

"I'm outside the church now. How long will it take for you to get here?"

"Caleb is getting dressed now, but he won't let us inside, not until after the coroner—"

She interrupted. "Never mind then. I'll tell you how it turns out."

I started to object but I was talking to a dead phone. Pearlie was doing exactly what I would do in her position.

I made the coffee and poked my head into the bathroom door long enough to tell Caleb I was going to the church, but not long enough to wait around to hear his objections. Jesse Jefferson was on our short list of suspects but he was the last person I would suspect of committing suicide.

~~~~~~~~~~

DPS officers were unrolling crime scene tape and tacking it to sawhorses as county sheriff deputies and city police urged an angry crowd to remain calm.

When I didn't see Pearlie, I used the excuse to ask a policeman if he'd seen Chief Stone yet.

"Over there, ma'am," he said, tipping his chin at Caleb's white and blue SUV pulling up to the curb.

Before he dipped under the yellow tape, I hitched my arm through his. "You forgot to shave," I said.

"What do you think you're doing?"

"Waiting for you," I said, grimly determined not to be left behind. "Let's see what's happened, shall we?"

Knowing he couldn't shake me off without making a scene, we walked into the church.

Two young sheriff's deputies were inside; one was holding a tall, metal, paint spattered ladder while another deputy, balanced on the highest step, was sawing at the rope.

Caleb rushed down the aisle, yelling at them to stop what they were doing. The young deputy with the saw turned to Caleb as the body slipped out of his grasp and fell the last few feet to the floor.

Caleb cursed. "What the hell do you think you're doing? This is a crime scene. Get off that damn ladder, now!"

I looked down at the pastor's normally cheerful dark face. His brown eyes were slightly open, the color faded in death to that of moonstones.

The rope had been thrown over one of the exposed rafters in front of the pulpit. The knot was clumsily done, but not everyone who kills themselves knows to use a hangman's knot that either breaks the neck as the weight of the body is dropped, or crushes the larynx, causing asphyxiation and death. This one seemed to have done the job, but I knew cause of death would still have to be determined by the M.E.

"Caleb," I said. "Ask them where the ladder was when they came into the church."

He was so angry I didn't think he'd be able to talk to these young men without choking one of them. "Was this ladder here when you came in?"

The deputy had been about to remove an altar cloth, but seeing chief's ice blue eyes go a shade colder, he gave it to the other deputy to cover the body. "I'm sorry, Chief Stone. We heard the call and got here as fast as we could. A crowd was gathering and I couldn't stand the thought of all those people seeing him like this."

"He's our pastor," the other deputy said.

"Just answer the question," Caleb said through clenched teeth.

"It was on the floor," he said, gulping nervously.

"How close to where he was hanging?" I asked.

"Just—I don't know, lying on the floor. About there, I guess," the young officer said, pointing a few feet away from where Jesse had been found hanging from a rafter.

That would work for a suicide if he kicked it over, but it didn't explain the gash on the back of the man's head.

"Who called it in?" Caleb asked.

The officer pointed to a weeping woman standing by the side door. "His missus."

"Did you call the medical examiner? Yes? Well there's one thing you did right. One of you take the front door, the other watch the side door and don't let *anyone* but the M.E. or Sheriff Tom inside, you understand?"

"Yes, sir," they said, and trotted for their assigned positions.

"Will you give me a few minutes to talk to Mrs. Jefferson?" I asked, unable to keep the sorrow out of my voice.

He held up five fingers and left. He understood that I was likely to get more out of the pastor's wife than he would right now. But this was his jurisdiction and his investigation and anything I learned would go directly to him, verbatim if necessary.

I nodded and left to hug Jesse's wife.

"Mrs. Jefferson, I'm so sorry," I said. "Do you want me to call someone for you?"

Her skin was grey, and in spite of the rising heat of summer, her hands were cold. She was going into shock.

"Let's go outside," I said, turning her for the door and away from the sight of her husband's black dress shoes sticking out from under a purple cloth.

I gently sat her down on a bench in the courtyard and rubbed her cold hands between mine. "Breathe, dear lady."

She threw her head back, gulping in great draughts of air as tears coursed down her dark cheeks. "Will you look at that? The sky is still blue, the sun is still shining. That's what my Jesse would call a good day."

"Do you have children or relatives we can call for you?"

"We never had chil'ren, all our relatives is in Mississippi, but don't you worry, honey, someone called my church ladies. They'll be here soon."

Seeing our time would soon be cut short, I asked, "Was there anything different, today or yesterday?"

"He always has a lot on his mind," she said, accepting the tissue I handed her. "Far as I could see, it weren't no different than any other day."

"Did you see him this morning?"

"No, but he a'ways is an early riser. Me, I like my coffee and a bit of TV in the mornin'. Jesse goes to his office for some prayer time before he answers e-mails and calls from folks in need. I don't usually see him until he comes home for suppa."

"How about problems with one of the congregation, or money problems?"

Mrs. Jefferson choked out a laugh. "We don't worry about such things, honey. If Jesse had extra, it would go into helpin' someone who needed it more. No, we used to livin' simple. But now that you mention it, his prayin' lately had been on someone special. He'd only say that he was wrestlin' with a problem that needed prayer. And then I found this." She held out a crumbled scribbled note.

Surprised, I read it and asked, "This is your husband's handwriting?"

"Looks like he wrote in a hurry, but yes, it's his," she said, blowing her nose on a tissue, "I don't have no idea what it means."

The words were scrawled in a quick motion, the pressure of the pen deep into the paper, as if he'd held the paper on his knee when he wrote it. It said, "*I tried to save them. Geronimo*...." Then nothing.

"Where did you find this?"

"In his pocket."

"What made you think to look in his pocket?"

"Oh, honey, I done washed that man's clothes for near on twenty years and I always turn out the pockets to collect the coins and such before they can get inta the spin cycle. He was forever writing on scraps of paper, scripture for this sermon or that and sometimes little snippets from the Song of Solomon," she stopped and tried to swallow, tears gathering in her eyes. "He knew I'd find them. Those little love notes always brightened my washday, that's for sure." She accepted the dry tissue. "Thanks, honey. Sweetest man ever born, my Jesse."

"If you don't mind," I said, standing, "I'll give this to Chief Stone."

"You take it, honey," she said, patting my hand as if I were the one in need of comfort. "It doesn't have anything to do with me."

Two women rushed to gather Mrs. Jefferson into their arms; the praying and crying following me as I hurried back into the cool, dark interior of the sanctuary.

The medical examiner had arrived and Ian Tom and Caleb stood to one side quietly conversing.

Caleb reached out and drew me into the circle. "The M.E. will need to determine exact cause of death, but I've already told Ian about the nasty gash on the back of Jesse's head."

"Don't forget the ladder," I said, "which may or may not have been moved."

Caleb scrubbed at his buzz cut and explained about the position of the ladder.

"They know better than to touch a crime scene," Ian said. "They'll be reprimanded."

"Ian, they're young and both are parishioners of Jesse's church," I said.

Ian shook his head. "I know it must've been a shock seeing their pastor like that, but they're on duty and they know the rules. What else do we have?"

"Mrs. Jefferson said he'd been praying for someone special, and she gave me a note from his pocket," I said, handing it to Caleb. I explained about the pastor's habit of leaving wash-day love notes to his wife.

Ian looked down and pinched the bridge of his nose. "My wife used to leave things like that in my lunch box."

Caleb read the note and asked, "Do you have any idea what this means?"

"Not me," I said.

I was still having odd dreams, ones where I was underwater and trying to converse with the old Apache who always managed to work in a repeat of the name, *Geronimo*. And here it was again. But Caleb was frankly suspicious of dreams so I went with a question that had been bothering me.

"Ian, why *did* you put Jesse Jefferson on the list? His wife said he didn't care all that much about money."

Ian looked around as if someone might be listening. "Let's take this conversation outside."

"Right," Caleb said, turning for the front door.

We walked into the starkly bright sunlight and shouting from an angry mob.

When a rock whizzed by his head, Ian ducked and swore. "What the hell?"

A mike boom from one of Tucson's news channels angled out over our heads, catching me in the middle of saying, "What's gotten into these people?"

Caleb moved me behind his back, stepped forward and held up his hand. When the discontented mob quieted, he pitched his voice to be heard by the last person in the back.

"I don't know what you've heard, but I am confirming that our department is investigating the death of Pastor Jefferson. You will not hear anything more until we have something to report, so I am asking all of you to please go home and let us do our jobs!"

No one moved. The crowd appeared to be holding their collective breaths—or they were thinking of who to throw the next rock at.

Using the brief silence to get in a question, the reporter shouted, "Did Pastor Jefferson hang himself because he was responsible for the unsolved shooting at the Miracle Faith Church?"

That started the shouting all over again.

Stunned, Caleb and I exchanged glances. So this is why Jesse's church family was here. Someone had leaked the death as a suicide to the press. No wonder his parishioners were angry.

Caleb turned to Ian. "See if you can talk some sense into this crowd. I'm going to get some smoke guns."

Caleb touched my elbow and I followed him to his SUV. He used his remote to unlock the doors and rummaging around the back, pulled out his megaphone and the smoke guns. Handing the smoke guns to me, he said, "I don't want to raise the level of paranoia, so give these to the patrolmen furthest away from the crowd, then go after that newsman. I think he's from a Tucson channel. Find out…"

"I'm on it," I said, and took off to find the Wishbone patrolmen. Reminding them of their chief's instructions, I headed for the brightly painted blue and white Channel 4 truck; complete with all the satellite equipment they would need for an instant upload to their TV station.

I yanked open the slider on the truck and scrambled inside. A driver, cameraman and a reporter were huddled around a monitor and jerked around in surprise at my bold entrance. I almost laughed at their fright—as if I might have a gun. Then again, this was Arizona where it's legal to carry a sidearm without a permit, but I wasn't. Not today, anyway.

"Shit," one of them said, reaching for the lock on the sliding door.

"If you're with the police, we have nothing to say," the one in the suit and tie said.

"I'm not with any law enforcement department," I said. "I'm a private investigator and I'm here to make a deal."

The cameraman and driver made noises that I should be kicked out, but the newsman hushed them with a wave of his hand, his eyes now squarely on mine.

"How'd you like to be first to get the whole story on the pastor's death?" I asked.

The cameraman smirked. "We already got that from the caller."

"Shut up, Dwayne," the newsman snarled.

Dwayne just confirmed my suspicions; the killer had made that call, bringing the reporter and crew all the way down here for the salacious details on a suicide. I could see the news bite now: *Popular pastor commits suicide as he's about to be exposed as a killer.*

That alone was enough for me to want to nip this in the bud. "I suppose your caller disguised his voice."

The cameraman snickered. "So what? Wouldn't you?"

The newsman threw up his hands. "Should we all just leave so you can tell the nice lady everything you know? Which won't be much because you're an idiot, Dwayne!"

The cameraman muttered under his breath, opened the sliding door and just before slamming it shut, said, "You think you're so smart. Well, I'm done with you, asshole!"

I listened to the A/C unit hum while the reporter thoughtfully rubbed his chin. Something told me he wasn't thinking about Dwayne.

"Nice rig," I said looking around.

"So it *was* murder, not suicide?" the newsman said, his eyes zeroing in on me.

I said yes because I didn't want the suicide angle to be part of the six-o-clock news. "But you don't have the full story," I said. "Not all of it."

"There's more?"

"When did you get the call about the pastor?"

The newsman was just young and hungry enough to see his advantage. "What do you think, Walt? Six a.m.? Yeah, about an hour before we got here."

The driver nodded. "That's what I remember."

"This is actually the second, and perhaps third, murder this week," I said. "And we believe they are all connected. We're this close," I said, holding up my thumb and forefinger about an inch apart, "to solving it."

The newsman undid his tie. "For such a quiet little town, bodies are dropping like flies; Ron Barbour, a local P.I. in a house explosion and big shot car dealer, Wade Hamilton, now missing and presumed dead. Who's the third? The pastor, right?"

I nodded. "What exactly did the caller say?"

"I can do better than that," he said, switching on a recording.

The voice was altered, but it was definitely male. "Pastor Jesse Jefferson hung himself this morning after investigators got a tip that he was responsible for a murder at the Miracle Faith Church shootout."

"Your turn," he said, crossing his arms and leaning back against the machinery.

"The police department got the call about the same time you did and before you ask, I know because I'm married to Wishbone's police chief. The pastor's hanging was meant to look like a suicide, but that was after someone bashed him in the back of the head."

The newsman stared for a minute. "Just enough titillating news to get us here. You said you're a private investigator? What's your interest in all of this?"

I chewed on my lip. Anything I said to him now would be used on the ten o'clock news, but wasn't that what I wanted? Turn up the heat on the killer. Smoke them out—or get myself killed trying.

"I can't tell you anything more than that I'm investigating a cold case murder that links all three of these dead men.

He rolled his eyes. "I can find the links by myself, but changing the subject, I'd be interested in your take on what I got in the mail last week."

My brows went up in question.

He waited, watching to see if I'd beg? I rolled my eyes at that idea and he said, "An unauthorized biography on Pastor Jefferson. Badly written, but the author claims that Jesse was slated to become Mother Beason's next bishop and that he never actually left the church. I figured it was simply hate mail, until today's phone call. Your turn."

"Who was the author?"

"Ronald T. Barbour."

When I flinched, he laughed. It was enough to let him know he'd hit a nerve. "Published by Office Max," he said, cheerfully.

"Was there a date on the publication?"

"I thought you'd never ask. A week ago today. I haven't the time or the resources to scour all of Tucson looking for which Office Max he used, but you're the investigator, right?"

Anyone can have a book printed these days. Had Ron written the one book in an attempt to blackmail the pastor? From everything I'd learned about Jesse, that idea was ridiculous. So what did Ron want? To ruin Jesse's career? The Ron I knew would've put aside any salacious information to be used later, like when Jesse was headed for bigger and better things.

The newsman cleared his throat, bringing me back to the moment. "I said, can I get your name? In case I have more questions?"

Now what was I going to tell him? That Pearlie and I were Ron Barbour's unsung business partners? I didn't have the time or the inclination. I smiled and said, "Susan Anthony."

One eyebrow went up. "Does that happen to come with the middle initial B?"

Busted, I opened the sliding door on the van to get out.

"Not even a card?" he asked, feigning disappointment. "Have it your way. We have footage of you in conversation with Wishbone's police chief. I'm sure someone in the newsroom can identify you."

I took his card, pocketed it, put my feet on the ground and said, "You'll get your story. All of it and soon, I promise."

~~~~~~~~~~~~~

Pearlie showed up as I was walking back to Caleb.

"Where've you been?" I asked.

"Ian Tom and Caleb are still doing crowd control and I got caught on the wrong side of the barricades. Boy, howdy, his parishioners are royally pissed. What have you learned?"

I told her about the anonymous call to the Tucson TV station and last, but not least, Jesse's unfinished note in his pocket.

"You still got the note?"

"No, I'm keeping my promise to be open and honest with my husband."

"In other words you turned it over to Caleb. I'm gonna write that down to remember should I ever get married."

"Oh yeah? When're you getting married?"

"Nothing happening on that front. I just want to remind myself to cut out all that stuff from my wedding vows."

"So which one of those bearded musician's did you go home with?"

"I had too much to drink, okay? Someone offered me a couch for the night and I took them up on it."

"Well then," I said. "You won't mind if we go see Harley Aldrich again today, will you?"

She rolled her lips inward, holding onto to her words so they wouldn't escape. Ha! Pearlie never could keep a secret from me.

I'd razz her about it, but right now we had work to do. "Let me tell Caleb we're leaving. Velma and Zelma are coming to the office at nine a.m."

"On a Sunday?" she asked. "Boy howdy, them girls' work ethics are showing real promise. Drop me off at my place. I'll pick up my Jeep and meet you at the office."

Chapter Twenty-four:

Ron's two ex-wives arrived as Pearlie and I were loading up more photos to show Harley. The women had ditched their black suits for colorful matching sundresses. Come to think of it, for sisters, they seemed remarkably similar in just about everything, including their need to get one up on the other. But then Pearlie and I had been scuffling with each other since we were kids. What was I saying? We were still hissing at each other, but I might as well ask.

They laughed and Zelma said, "We're fraternal twins."

"Though you wouldn't know it," Velma said, with a twinkle in her eye. "She looks so much older than me, doesn't she?"

Zelma hooted. "That's a good one. You got kids older than me."

I held up a hand to stop the arguing before it got out of hand. "Do either of you have any questions before we leave?"

"Well," Zelma said looking around at the drab office. "The place sure looks run-down. Don't you wonder what Ron did with his money?"

She was fishing, hoping we knew where he'd hidden his stash of get-out-of-town money. "We wondered about that too. His house sure wasn't anything to look at."

"We worked at a call center," Zelma said, "so you just want us to answer phones, take messages and that sort of thing?"

"What sort of thing?" Pearlie asked, looking up from sorting photos.

"We did phone surveys, questionnaires," Velma said.

"Really?" Pearlie laid her purse on the desk. "Then go through Ron's old accounts. Find the businesses that could use our services. Make a list to call on Monday."

The two women whipped out their matching notepads and started writing.

"We can ask them when was the last time they used Ron's services," Velma said.

"That's a good idea," Pearlie said with a wink at me.

"And if they quit Ron, you want to know why, right?" Zelma said.

I shuddered, wondering how many other people Ron tried to blackmail.

"And if they're using another P.I. firm," Velma said, "would a discount convince them to use you ladies as private investigators?"

"A discount?" I squeaked. "I don't think…"

Pearlie elbowed my ribs. "We'll take anything you can get, but make any appointments for a week from today."

By then, we'd know one way or the other if we would get our P.I. Licenses or our walking papers.

"By the way, what're you going to call your business?" Velma continued.

"It's Bains and Bains Private Investigations," I said with a straight face.

The twins giggled. "You sure you don't want to call it Two Blondes' Investigations?"

Pearlie nudged me. "Aren't they clever? And so close to my original suggestion of Two Blonde Jobs."

"No thanks," I said. "We're going to have enough problems getting companies to take us seriously."

As I closed the door behind me, I noticed the twins hungrily eyeing Ron's old file cabinets. I figured the minute the door closed, those two would start tearing up the place looking for the money Ron had looted from our business.

Taking the stairs down to the parking lot, Pearlie assured me that Harley could see us today.

We took separate cars to our meeting with Harley. Pearlie needed to do grocery shopping and I intended to stop by Wishbone's police station and see if Caleb had any more information on Jesse's murder.

Taking Highway 92 south, I passed the ruins of the Miracle Faith Bible Church. It reminded me that we were down by one more suspect. With Jesse dead and Wade Hamilton presumed dead, we were left with only Andy Sokolov and no witnesses other than a pitiful wheelchair bound woman.

It was only bad timing that prevented us from interviewing Jesse Jefferson. Someone had to have known we were about to ask him questions. There was nothing in the file that said he was ever a member of the Faith Miracle Church. Had he become a minister as penance for his crime? Or was he the one person with proof against the other two? If so, Jesse's reputation as an honest pastor would've sealed Andy's and Wade's fate.

I looked in the rear view mirror at Pearlie. Following anyone, much less me, was not her strong suit. She preferred to be in front and ahead of me—in everything. Well, she could pass me up anytime she wanted.

But she'd been right about the twin sisters; they were just what we needed. The idea of new business in Ron's old client list was a stroke of genius. We'd find Ron's killer, wrap Damian's case and have new business waiting for us when we got our licenses approved by the state.

If we got our licenses. It would work. It had to work. Yes, that's the way to think. I wouldn't worry about it today. Worrying about this today was the sledge hammer to failure. That much I knew to be true. I'll think about it tomorrow. Or as Dr. Phil would say, *so how's that working out for you, Scarlett?*

~~~~~~~~~~~

Today's summer rain had brightened the sky and greened up the hills behind Harley Aldrich's home, making the multi-hued paint job on his house stand out like a pop art poster for psychedelic drugs.

We parked and took the path to his front door, but hearing the buzz of a gas powered saw, I hesitated. "Sounds like he's cutting wood. What if he doesn't remember us?"

Pearlie shrugged and led the way to the back of the house

He had on a straw hat, no shirt and a pair of faded and ripped tight jeans. He couldn't hear us over the saw, so Pearlie put out a hand to stop me from trying to speak over the noise. She winked, grinned and patted the spot over her heart as she watched the muscles ripple across Harley's sweaty back.

Feeling like a silly voyeur, I decided to stop Pearlie's peep show and called to him. "Hello, Harley!"

"Ah, you're no fun," Pearlie said, smacking me on the arm.

He put the gas saw in neutral, waved back and shut off the saw. He removed his work gloves and waited.

"I don't think he recognizes us," I said. "I hope we won't have to start all over again."

Pearlie snorted and held out her hand. "Hi Harley, remember me?"

He took her hand in his and drew her to him. "Pearlie. How could I ever forget *you*?"

She laughed and put a hand on his broad chest to push him away. "And you need a shower, Harley Aldrich."

Well, well. Harley's facial recognition didn't interfere with his ability to play the fiddle with my cousin. And I never did get to pin her down on how she ended up in Wishbone so early this morning. Maybe he was right, all those photos and descriptions on the walls were just so he could keep in practice.

Harley, keeping Pearlie's hand, looked at me and asked, "Who's your friend?"

Okay, so I was wrong again.

"Oh, don't tease her. Let's go inside. You got any lemonade?"

He laughed. "Okay, sorry. Hi Lalla. Just let me hang up this saw and I'll be right with you."

"So how did he do that?"

"We'll talk about it later. You got the photos?"

"Of course."

Harley insisted on serving us lemonade and another plate of his homemade cookies. "Excuse me for a few minutes? I've got woodchips in my hair and if I don't go clean up, it'll be all over the house in no time."

When he left for the bathroom, I asked, "How does he do it?"

"He told you how he does it. Remember the first thing he said to me was that I smelled good? His sense of smell is so heightened that it all comes back to him the minute you get close to him. That and the fact that you were with *me*. He's not stupid, you know."

It was clever of him, but I was looking forward to testing out Harley's memory of the one person he hadn't identified from the earlier pictures. "I thought you didn't like him?"

"Don't go putting words in my mouth. I never said that."

"Okay, but I thought you were dating the homicide detective?"

"That's off. He won't share anything on Ron's murder case, much less the covers. I knew I was right about that man."

"Then you and Harley, huh?"

She shrugged. "He'd have to shave that horrible bush off his face and I doubt he'd do that even for me."

Harley came back, buttoning up a clean shirt. "Would you be satisfied with a trim?"

Unwilling to listen to Pearlie backpedal, I said, "We've brought more photos of the shootout."

Harley listened, but his attention was on Pearlie. "You're rushing over parts of this because you think I won't remember, right? Let me help you out. I remember most everything. It's new people, new faces, okay?"

"Right. Got it," I said, fanning the photos over his coffee table. "Do any of these people look familiar?"

"Sure," he said. There's Ted Moskel and Danny Oaks, Marvin... uh, forgot his last name, but Marvin went into the Marines and came back pretty messed up. Now he lives on the street and everyone just calls him Marvin the can man. I give him all my cans to sell. Okay, so you brought me some new photos. That's Andy Sokolov," he said. "He used to be a deputy sheriff, but now he's the mayor of Wishbone. I don't know this guy," he said, pointing to a picture of Ron Barbour. He shuffled through the photos and picked up the picture of Jesse Jefferson, "I saw this man at the shootout, but I don't know his name."

"Was he behind the barricades, or with someone?" I asked.

"I'm not sure. He wasn't in the last photos you showed me, but he was there. Wait. Now I remember. I saw him pull a woman and her little boy away from the fight. I remember because her long braid was coming loose and she was crying. I wondered what happened to her and the kid. Then the shooting started and the police pushed all of us out of the way."

"Most of the women in the church wore head scarves. Are you sure her hair was in a braid and not covered, Harley?" Pearlie asked.

He tilted up his head and worked a forefinger around the back of his head as if feeling for a braid. "She was different. Much prettier than the other women and her hair was black, but it was definitely a braid, not a scarf. I also remember that her skin was a coppery color. Well then, she was Native American?"

"This was Damian's mother?" I asked Pearlie.

"Who?" Harley asked.

Pearlie said, "She's the only native American we know of associated with the church. But how did she know Jesse Jefferson?"

"We can talk about that later," I said, standing. "I need to go by the police station and see Caleb."

"Wait," Harley said holding up a photo. "You forgot to ask me about this one. It's your shooter. He's older and he wasn't in a deputy's uniform, but this is your guy."

Wade Hamilton's toothy smile smiled at us from his publicity picture. "Are you sure he wasn't in uniform?" I asked.

Pearlie slapped my arm. "If he said Wade wasn't in uniform on the day of the shooting, then he's sure, aren't you, honey?"

Now her empathy meter was working? I decided to leave it for later.

"Did I help?" Harley said, getting to his feet.

"Yes, you did, sweetums," Pearlie said, squeezing his hard bicep.

I swept up the pile of pictures and stood.

"Are you leaving already? I was going to make lunch. Pearlie?"

"I'll be right back," she said, touching Harley's cheek.

I rushed her outside and gushed, "That's it, then. Wade Hamilton was the shooter."

"Sure we have a name, but if you will remember, Harley's testimony would be inadmissible in court."

"But… "

"I'm staying," she said, her hand on the door knob. "Harley fixes the best chicken salad and he's got fresh homemade bread."

"All right," I said, feeling my earlier euphoria slide into oblivion. "I'll see you at the office after lunch."

~~~~~~~~~~~~~

I grabbed the bag of sandwiches I'd bought at Cornucopia Café on Main Street, then drove to Wishbone's police station. Counting myself lucky to find a guest parking spot, I positioned the requisite sunshades across the front windows, then cracked the driver's side window to allow the hot air to escape, scooted around a couple of officers jawing about a recent ball game and stepped through the entrance.

Rapping on the window to get Betty's attention, she came around to open the door for me. "Hi Lalla, go on back."

I thanked her, turned into the hall and knuckled the frame on his open door. "I've got lunch," I said, holding up the two paper bags.

The skin around his light blue eyes crinkled happily.

"Outside?" I asked.

"Someone put the umbrella up on the patio set out back and I could use the break."

"Have you been at your desk all morning?" I asked, opening the bag and parceling out the turkey, avocado and cheese sandwiches. I licked at a dollop of avocado and sighed happily. I loved lunch at Cornucopia. I'd eat there every day, but then I'd gain weight.

"Fielding reporter's questions, mostly," he said, chewing.

"Can you get out of here this afternoon?" I asked. "I want to talk to Naomi White and I'd like you to go with me."

"Today? I'd like to. Where's she live?"

"It's off Highway 10, up Texas Canyon, at the turn-off for the Amerind Museum."

"We should go back there when they have the Chiricahua celebrations."

"Sometime soon, I think. I'll call the museum. So what do you think? Can you get away?"

He tilted his head. "Wasn't that where you lost the Alzheimer's patient?"

Yes, I'd been in the area recently. Hours of trekking in the cold and dark and I've been dreaming about him ever since. "Yes. Same area. Can you come? I'll fill you in on what we learned about Pastor Jefferson."

Caleb understood that for me, this would be revisiting a site I'd just as soon forget. "Give me five minutes to clear my calendar and I'll go with you."

"Great," I said sweeping the crumbs and wrappers into the lunch bag. "My Jeep or your SUV?" I asked, hoping I could avoid another tank of gas on my no salary job.

He patted my cheek as he passed. "We'll take my ride. It's official business, isn't it?

Chapter Twenty-five:

On the drive to Naomi White's home near the Dragoons, I told Caleb that Harley Aldrich identified Jesse Jefferson helping Naomi and her son escape the shooting.

Caleb nodded. "I think everyone knew Jesse was helping church members get out of that cult, but if he was there to help Naomi and Damian escape, someone besides a twelve-year-old kid must've seen them."

"I can think of two people who might've seen him: Wade Hamilton and Andy Sokolov. And I've got a theory. Either Jesse shot Damian's dad and the other two have been keeping his secret. Or one of the other two killed the dad and Jesse agreed to keep it a secret because he was there helping Naomi get away from her husband."

"Naomi White has been interviewed several times by Homicide and so far she's never admitted to having any connection to Jesse or Wade or Andy."

I was thinking of my search and rescue partner's comment about how reticent Native Americans are to give up information, especially to local law enforcement. Left with only speculation, we followed the interstate highway east into Texas Canyon. Erosion has scoured away the dirt, leaving boulders stacked one on top of the other, looking like a giant had deliberately placed them there just to please visitors. My favorite time to drive through the Texas canyon was when the late afternoon sun flamed the stacked rocks red and left the others in shades of lavender.

Taking the turnoff for the little hamlet of Dragoon, we passed the Amerind Museum, reminding ourselves to come back for a visit.

Forty minutes later and a wrong turn that ended at a locked gate, we found the entrance to Naomi White's place. Passing under a striking metal arch of interwoven arrow-heads, I felt I should know the place.

"Could it be the same property?"

"I didn't go to the man's house, or meet his daughter. Besides, it's so dark out here everything outside of our headlights simply vanishes."

I caught a glimpse of an old weathered shack behind a triple-wide modular home. Next to it was a giant metal arrow someone had planted in the earth to look as if it had been shot from the quiver of the boulder stacking giants of Texas Canyon.

We knocked and the door was opened by an attractive woman in her late sixties, her graying hair pulled back into one long braid, her calloused hands gripping the collar of a very alert German Shepherd. Her eyes were large in her face, very dark and heavily fringed by thick straight lashes. Casually dressed in jeans and a simple white linen blouse, she managed to look elegant, her only jewelry consisting of multiple bracelets banding both wrists.

When she spoke, her voice was low and modulated in that way of someone whose English is a second language. "I was expecting a private investigator, not Wishbone's police chief. Is this an official visit, Chief Stone?"

"I have a couple of questions that you can help with," Caleb responded. "May we come in?"

"Of course," she said, lowering her eyes so that the thick lashes lay artfully against the high cheekbones. She gave a soft command and the dog trotted over to a bed of old blankets, curled up and with head on paws, kept us in his line of sight.

Lifting a languorous hand she waved us inside.

The interior of her home was sparsely furnished with a coffee table in front of a sofa. There was no TV, but an iPad was hooked up to a couple of small speakers and Native American flute music softly played.

On the wall were framed magazine covers with her picture and several framed award ribbons from Native American jewelry contests. In striking contrast to Andy's wheelchair bound accuser there were no photos of her son, Damian. Not on the walls or in frames on her mantle. I thought it telling of this woman's character, or maybe I was making too much of it.

The rest of the living room was devoted to a long workbench, tools and boxes of supplies. It all looked costly, but Ian did say she made a good living at it.

"The bracelets you're wearing are lovely, are they your designs?" I asked.

She held out her arm for me to see, laying a slender, tanned finger on one silver and turquoise cuff. "Only this one. The others are gifts from friends."

She pointed to her workbench and showed us her tools. "This is a sand cast for silver. I draw my design, work it in clay and then carve it from Utah sandstone. It is very soft to carve and gives a wonderful natural look to the silver, but like a lot of things in this life, it doesn't last very long."

"The boxes," I asked. "What's in those?"

She folded her hands in front of her and in that softly modulated voice said, "I keep silver and stones in those boxes against the wall. A photo on the front of each box describes what's inside. Silver birds, buttons, various sizes, shapes, The colored stones I put in alphabetical order: fluorite, malachite, opal, tanzanite, tourmaline and turquoise."

"I hope you have security for your home," Caleb said.

"I have security lights," Naomi said, "but if there are intruders bent on theft I have Artemis over there on his bed and a loaded rifle I keep by the door."

She glanced down at her calloused hands and then up through the proud dark eyes. "I was already interviewed by Detective Hutton. I have an alibi for the day Ron Barbour was killed. Then again, why would I want to kill him? I paid good money for him to find my husband's killer."

Caleb said, "Your interview with Sierra Vista Homicide said that you were at a jewelry show in Phoenix. I'm more interested in where you were this morning."

Her chin lifted, a defiant gesture meant to show that she wasn't going to be cowed by the likes of a police chief. "I don't have an alibi for this morning, Chief Stone. I was here all day, alone, so there is no one to vouch for me."

"All right," I said. "But you knew Pastor Jefferson, didn't you?"

Her head came up and her response to my question wasn't answered at once, but in an instant her demeanor morphed into that of someone softer, weaker, as if she had been crushed by circumstances beyond her control.

Her arm came up again to indicate that we should sit.

Caleb and I took the sofa and waited for her to continue.

She stared at her hands while she talked. "I was seventeen when I met Damian's father. He was stationed at Ft. Huachuca and about to be transferred to an Army base in

DC, so we married. Unfortunately, that's where he met Mother Beason and her Miracle Faith Church. Her sermons about the repressed and downtrodden clicked with him but not me. I could not believe he could be taken in by the woman's lies, but then he revered my shaman father, too." She stopped talking, her eyes apparently interested in the shape of her fingers.

"But you came back to Arizona with your husband?" I asked to keep her talking.

"Only after I found out I was pregnant. I had my son and things were better for a while, but then the trouble started between the police and the church. Jesse Jefferson knew that I wanted out, but I couldn't find a way to leave without my husband threatening to kill me. By the time the deputies came, church members were lined up with rifles and shotguns refusing to allow anyone to come onto the property.

"With my suitcase and my son, I ran for Jesse's car. But my husband saw us and aimed his rifle at us. He was willing to murder his own son if it kept me from leaving. He would've too, but thank God someone else shot him first. Whoever shot him saved my life and maybe my son's as well."

"Does Damian know the details of that day?" I asked.

"I told Damian how his father died, but he's determined to find his father's killer."

"What's to say the man who shot Damian's father hasn't moved away? Or maybe he's already dead?"

"I believe Ron Barbour had a name," she said, quietly.

Ron could've been lying to get her money. There were plenty of times when he'd done exemplary work as an investigator, just not in the last few years.

"Have you and Pastor Jefferson kept in touch?"

I was surprised to see annoyance momentarily flash in her eyes. "I could never repay Jesse for what he did for me and my son, but after that day, we moved back here and I never saw him again."

Her words didn't match the look, but I wasn't about to call her on it now so instead I kept my questions to something less confrontational. "Did you live here with your father?"

She hesitated, glancing around the room as if looking for someone who should be there.

"I returned to live here when my husband died. This was my father's property but he wouldn't have anything to do with living in my new home. He had dementia, so I shouldn't have been surprised. He forgot what day it was and some days he did not even know me. Then a few days ago, when he was completely lucid, he walked away."

Now I felt a chill run over my skin. "How did he die?"

The woman's black eyes went darker as she thoughtfully appraised me. "He took his ceremonial costume, led a search and rescue team all the way up to the Cochise Stronghold, then leaped to his death, right in front of them."

Caleb and I exchanged a glance. I hadn't seen Ian Tom that night, but as Cochise County's sheriff, he would have been with the first responders, yet he never mentioned his relationship to the old man.

"I was part of that search and rescue team," I said, trying to cover my shock. "He said something as he went over, but I couldn't understand it. My team partner speaks some Navajo and he thought it might've been Apache."

Naomi's dark eyes gave me a thorough going over. "He spoke to you?"

"Well, sort of, but like I said...."

She moved a hand impatiently. "Did he speak to any-one else?"

"Uh-well, I don't think so. I'm still not sure why he chose to say anything to me."

Her eyes raked mine as if trying to understand the for-eign language I was speaking. "And now you dream of him."

My breath caught in my throat. "I-I, well, uh, I think it was the shock of seeing him leap to his death in front of us."

She leaned forward, her eyes now wide with interest. "I am not a religious person. The old ways of my people seem childish and I hated my husband's fanatical church. I didn't listen when my father warned me of the trouble that would come of marrying. I thought he was just trying to keep me away from the man I loved. When I moved back here, he chose to live in the shack behind the house and we did not talk much. Yet, in your dreams he speaks to you. What does he say?"

"Nothing really. It was only two or three times. I think. In one dream, I'm sitting on the bottom of a lake, or maybe it's the ocean, which is weird since apparently I could breathe underwater. He sticks his head into the water and tries to speak, but of course, he can't, so he sputters and withdraws."

"Perhaps he is trying to tell you something."

"I should stay away from water?" I said, trying to make light of it.

"Perhaps," she said, and moved away from me.

Perhaps with her father's death she was having a religious reawakening and I had offended her. Until this minute, I'd forgotten about my own long dead mother rousing me from a drugged sleep so that I could escape from a burning house. This felt different and yet it wasn't. I guess I should start paying attention to my dreams.

~~~~~~~~~~

On the way home, Caleb warned me against doing any such thing.

"Why do you say that?"

"Because you get sidetracked from the main issue."

"I think there's a reason why I continue to dream about him," I said.

"I think it's due to the shock of seeing him go over that cliff. So what did you think of her story?"

He was trying to pull me back on track.

"Oh, well," I said, thoughtfully. "For one thing, she doesn't strike me as the helpless type."

"Who said she was helpless?"

"Ian did," I said. "You were there. He said she was fragile, remember?"

"There's Gabby Hayes's account of the abusive husband," he said.

"Yes. Didn't you find it strange that there were no pictures of Damian? Only pictures of herself and her jewelry awards. What mother doesn't have photos of their only child?"

"What're you getting at?" he asked.

"Her brother said she was fragile, Jesse saves her from an abusive husband and someone else, maybe Wade Hamilton, or Andy Sokolov shot the man they saw as a monster ready to kill his own wife and son. What if this was what she meant when she told Gabby that she had her own plans for her husband?"

"You think she hired one of them to shoot her husband?"

"Hired? Oh, no I don't think so. She was young, very beautiful, still is for that matter. An affair between her and one of the men could've taken care of that problem. Or," I said, considering another angle, "what if she was the one with the rifle? She owns one and admitted being a competent shooter. So she hands Jesse the weapon and tells him it's her only chance to be free, once and for all."

"Someone had to have seen it happen. How was it kept secret?"

"I think that's why Ian came up with these three names: Wade Hamilton, Andy Sokolov and Jesse Jefferson. He knew, or suspected that these three men had something to do with the shooting."

"It's easy to hypothesize when two out of three of the suspects are dead or missing."

"You're right, but Pearlie and I have already come up with totally new leads; Harley Aldrich, Wade Hamilton's ex-bookkeeper and last but not least, Andy Sokolov's accuser. As for Naomi, we only have her word for it—that her husband was abusive and pointed a rifle at her and her child."

"Lalla, if any of this is true, she's not going to admit anything that will incriminate her now."

"But Ron's and Jesse's murders are recent, which brings me to believe that whoever is left is our killer. And there're the dreams. Two times with the water dream. I can't figure what that was about. Then the name Geronimo keeps popping up."

"I think you're stressing yourself out over this case."

"Can't argue with that. Have you heard from the M.E. on the cause of death for Jesse?"

"He was unconscious but alive when he was strung up over that rafter."

"From the gash on the back of his head?"

"More like smashed," he said, touching the spot near the base of his skull to show me. "It takes some strength to do that kind of damage. I think we can safely rule out Naomi."

Someone came up on him from behind, struck him on the back of the head, then carted him into the church and strung him up. Jesse wasn't a big man, but his murder had to be done by a man; someone strong enough to be able hoist his unconscious body up by a rope. "Why bother trying to make it look like a suicide when the M.E. was just going to declare it a murder anyway? What about time of death?"

"Lividity corresponds with an early a.m. death."

"I think it's time we talked to Ian about this. Will you call him?"

He looked at his watch. "It's late. I'll call him tomorrow. Maybe we can meet for lunch, will that do?"

"Yes," I said, wishing I didn't now feel suspicious of Ian's motives. Did he know or suspect Naomi's involvement with Jesse? What else was Ian not telling us?

"You said Ian was tapping their cell and home phones?" I asked.

"Yes, but unfortunately, Andy has his Google location tracker turned off."

"How convenient for him. Do we have ours on or off?"

He gave me a look that indicated I shouldn't have to ask. "Sweetheart. Better than hanging a bell around your neck, isn't it? If you disappeared it might be the only way I'd have to find you."

"And is yours on?"

"Always, I'm a cop."

Chapter Twenty-six:

I awoke tired from a restless night. Sometime this week we'd get a notice from the State Board of Licensing telling us we were out of business. We'd also lose access to the internet tools we needed to continue as a P.I. firm. Dead in the water, a phrase that suited not only our future as P.I.'s, but also my unsettling dreams.

Caleb left for work and I got into the shower. As the hot water streamed over my back, I thought of last night's underwater dream. It was a lake rather than the ocean, wasn't it? Both places have tiny fish and sand on the bottom, but there was something else. Ah, yes, a beer can. Not just any brand, but the popular Mexican Tecate, like what Ian offered us when we first went to his home. Was this just my imagination running amok or was there a clue here I was missing? A lake. Wade Hamilton's last known sighting was at Lake Patagonia. Maybe it was time for me to revisit the place. I would do that right after I went back to see what Mrs. Jefferson had to say about a fourth suspect.

I went to the office, greeted Zelma and Velma and called Pearlie, but when her cell went to message, I looked at my watch. It was barely nine a.m. and Pearlie was a night owl. I left a message, told her where I was going and why.

~~~~~~~~~~~

Mrs. Jefferson insisted I join her for a cup of coffee. "My morning routine seems to be all that's holding me together. Cream or sugar?"

I thanked her and accepted mine black. When we were both seated, I brought out the photos and spread them on the coffee table. "Do you know any of these people?"

"Well, of course, honey. That's the mayor, Andy Sokolov. He and his missus come to Easter and Christmas services, and this is Ian Tom. Ian and his wife used to come every Sunday until the cancer took her, poor woman. This picture looks like his sister. I think her name is Naomi? Yes, that's it. Nice woman, quiet, rather shy. Ian brought her a few times. Now, Wade Hamilton I know 'cause his face is on a local TV channel every night trying to convince folks that, 'Nobody beats a Hamilton deal.' But since he's not up for re-election I never see him in church."

When she saw my blush, she reached over and patted my hand. "Now, honey, don't you give it another thought. Of course, it looks good for the chief of police to attend services here. Jesse and I knew that and it wasn't so awful bad for our image, either."

"Thank you, Mrs. Jefferson," I said, putting the photos back into the envelope. Then I thought of something else. "You said Pastor Jefferson counseled people in the mornings. Did he ever counsel Ian's sister, Naomi White?"

"Well now, Jesse kept his own appointments. Let's go to his office and look at his calendar."

Mrs. Jefferson led me along a walkway until we came to a modular trailer with a sign on the door that said, *Pastor's Office*. She unlocked the door and ushered me inside. "We got robbed once, can you imagine? We don't have a lock on our own house, but Jesse had to lock his office."

She walked around his desk, muttering at the growing pile of mail. "Jesse didn't hold with fancy appointment books. He made all of his on this here desk calendar," she said, handing it to me.

I looked for the day of his murder, but this month's page had been ripped off. "Did the police perhaps remove this month's sheet for evidence?"

She shook her head, looking around the office as if seeing it for the first time. "Honey, I don't rightly know. It's all been a blur since he died. I-I can't hardly stand coming in here no more."

"We can leave," I said, gently guiding her out of the office. Taking the key from her hand, I locked the door and noticed that there were scratch marks on the keyhole.

Someone had broken in. Before or after Jesse was killed? I remember the morning we were called to the church. Caleb was beside himself trying to secure a crime scene that was getting out of hand. Way too many people coming and going; police, Mrs. Jefferson's church ladies, reporters and the TV vans and last but not least, Ian Tom.

~~~~~~~~~~~~

It was still early. I had plenty of time to get to the lake where I would sort out my theory, but I needed just one more visit to ask Harley if he would confirm one last identity.

He was working in his garden, hat on, shirt off, the bushy beard recently barbered. Now all of his handsome face could be seen. I only hoped Pearlie appreciated the concessions he was making for her.

He wiped his hands on his faded jeans and smiled. "Hello, Lalla Bains," he said, looking past me to the Jeep. "Pearlie not with you this time?"

No wonder this man had so many friends. Harley's inability to hide his feelings was so endearing that I was tempted to hug him. "Hello, Harley. No, sorry, too early for Pearlie."

"Well, maybe later today," he said. "Coffee? I still have a pot on if you like."

"I'm good, but thanks," I said, pulling out the photos I'd shown to Mrs. Jefferson and spreading them out on the kitchen counter. Harley remembered our last meeting, so I separated the photos I'd shown him a few days ago from the new ones.

"Okey dokey," he said, rubbing his hands together. "Andy Sokolov and several other men I know were sheriff deputies and they were at the shooting, but not the shooter." He pointed to a figure in the photo. "This is the sheriff of Cochise County." At my look of surprise, he laughed. "I don't remember the face but I know the uniform."

"It's Sheriff Ian Tom. He moved back to the area to be close to his family about eight years ago."

"Thanks for that. I'll write down his name so I can greet him properly when we meet. And this is...," he said, thoughtfully tapping the publicity photo of Naomi White. "She's older now, but this is the woman I saw running away with Jesse Jefferson."

I smiled my thanks and put away the photos.

"What does it mean?" he asked, as I prepared to leave. "Does the woman have anything to do with your murder investigation?"

"That's something I'm going to have to find out, Harley."

~~~~~~~~~~~

I drove from Wishbone along Highway 92, passing the falling down buildings that had been the scene of Cochise County's fatal interaction with a religious cult. I took the Buffalo Soldier Trail, by-passing Sierra Vista and then it was a straight shot north on Highway 92 until a left turn onto Highway 82. Now it was all open range, fenced at the highway, homes and ranches dotting the dry and rolling landscape. I passed through the little town of Sonoita where Santa Cruz County fairgrounds held the state's oldest horse races and then slowed again at the small artsy town Patagonia and then made a right turn into Patagonia State Park.

I paid the fee and parked in the day use parking lot. Since it was Monday, only a few fishermen stood along the deep end of the lake, their lines dipping under the calm surface of the water. Two nodded a greeting as I passed, lifting me out of my somber mood with the pleasantries. I had made the right decision, coming out here where I could sort through the facts about this case.

I hiked uphill to the day camp area. A skinny old man smelling of stale cigarettes and old fish, climbed out of the bushes and passed me. He glanced up in surprise at my friendly greeting then tugged the brim of his hat down over his face. I guess not everyone at the lake was happy to greet a newcomer.

I got as far as the path went before it ran out of macadam and into a wall of rock. While I considered going back or climbing over, I heard someone calling my name.

I turned and saw Damian and Pearlie in the parking lot. I waved back and cupped my ears to hear what she was trying to say. Why didn't she just call me on her cell? And why was Damian with her? I looked at my cell—oh. No bars, no cell phone service. I took a step in their direction and felt the business end of a gun stick into my side. "Keep your hands where I can see them and don't try anything."

My hands instinctively jerked into the air while Pearlie's hands dropped down to her sides.

I turned and looked at the man with the gun. The grubby old fisherman I'd surprised was Wade Hamilton. He was thin to the point of emaciated, unshaven and looking every bit as if he'd been living rough. The shock of seeing him here didn't do much for my attempt to deceive him. "Mr. Hamilton? Where have you been? People are looking for you."

Wade reached out and shoved me toward Pearlie and Damian. "Shut up and keep moving." He walked me along the edge of the road, keeping me in front of him and Pearlie in his line of sight.

"Wave to them. Smile," he said.

I did as I was told, but changed tactics. "Your wife will be thrilled to hear that you're alive, sir. You can call her with my cell, if you like."

"My wife is the last person I'd want to talk to right now," he growled. "Besides, reception sucks."

He had that right. "Then why are you hiding out here?"

Wade's high-pitched cackle was pretty far off his usual swaggering TV persona, but a week without decent food or shelter could do that.

"You really don't know, do you? She followed you here. I saved her and this is the thanks I get. We'll take your car."

I looked to where Pearlie and Damian stood waiting. Pearlie had her hand in the zippered compartment that held her pistol. Wade would have to be delusional if he thought my cousin was going to let him get the better of her.

"You don't have to be afraid of your wife, Wade."

"Shut up and walk," he said, shoving the handgun into my ribs again. There was no mistaking his anxious need to keep moving.

With my eyes on Pearlie and Damian, I was hoping for a way to distract him so that Pearlie could shoot him in the leg, or shoulder—as long as she didn't shoot me, but then I heard the sharp report of a rifle.

I felt Wade stumble against me, his eyes wide as he grabbed for me. I tried to shove him away, but he wouldn't let go.

We fell off the path and rolled downhill toward the deep end of the lake. Seeing the water come up on us, I grabbed a lungful of air, squeezed my eyes shut and waited for the impact. I kicked and flailed to get him off, but Wade's heavy body stubbornly remained on top, driving the reserve out of my lungs, forcing us under. Deeper and deeper until I felt the useless air slip out of my mouth. I fought to stay conscious, but my limbs were now numb and my vision was closing into a small circle of light. I struggled to get my feet under me so I could push off, but I was so weak. A Tecate can lay next to my hand and above me a dead man floated away.

That's when I heard the old Apache speak to me. "Save the boy."

Chapter Twenty-seven:

Someone was beating on my chest and calling my name, but when I tried to tell them to stop, it all came out in a rush of water. I rolled over on my side and threw up again and again, relieved laughter following the purge.

"It's rude to laugh at a drowning victim," I muttered.

Pearlie snickered and pulled me up into a sitting position. "Good thing Damian was quick to dive in and pull you out when he did. His CPR ain't so bad, either."

Damian. The boy. Three words. The words I couldn't get right, *Save the boy.* That's what the old Apache said as he went over the cliff, and Damian was the old man's grandson. Ironically, I didn't save the boy, the boy saved me.

"Wade," I coughed. "Where is he?"

"Over there," Pearlie pointed to where Damian, in T-shirt and white Jockey shorts, was tugging Wade's heavy body up onto the sandy bank.

I shivered and clenched my jaw to keep my teeth from chattering. "D-did you shoot him?" I asked.

"I'm good with a pistol, but not at that range. It had to be a rifle and it came from behind those trees. And don't bother to ask if we saw him, we were too busy trying to save you."

Damian looked up and waved.

I pushed my wet hair out of my eyes and struggled to get on my feet.

"Easy does it," Pearlie said, giving me a hand up. "You almost drowned, you know."

"But I didn't," I said, wrapping my arms around myself to keep from shivering. "Wade said *she* followed him out here. I thought he meant you."

"About the same time I got your message, Damian showed up at the office and I decided to bring him along. I was thinking you might be looking for Wade," Pearlie said, "but it never occurred to me that he'd find you first. Someone else was looking for him, too?"

"Yes," I croaked and coughed. My voice was painfully scratchy from my near drowning.

She looked over her shoulder at the trees behind us. "Bet you five bucks it was a rifle."

"Yes. I thought so, too." The pieces were starting to come together. "Steve said they're the best trackers in the West."

"You are not making any sense. Did you crack your head when you went under?"

"Wade said he *saved* her and this was the thanks he got. I think Wade Hamilton is the deputy who shot Damian's father, thinking he was protecting a woman and a child running for their lives."

"You talking about Ian's sister, Naomi? What makes you think she's the shooter?"

In spite of the warm day, I was still wet. That and the shock of discovery was making my teeth clack like castanets. "I-I'll tell you later. N-no time. Call 9-1-1, then Caleb."

"You're shivering. Come with me to the Jeep and get warm."

"N-not yet. Bring back a blanket to cover the b-body. I have t-to talk to Damian." Seeing she was about to argue, I gave her a shove. "No time. Go. I'll meet you in the parking lot, I promise."

Pearlie reluctantly agreed, stopping long enough to congratulate Damian on a job well done, then fast walk for the main parking lot and a clear cell phone signal.

Damian had managed to pull on dry pants over his wet legs, but he had his cross-trainers in one hand. "We heard the shot that got him," he said. "Who did it?"

If Wade hadn't fallen into me, forcing both of us into the lake, she might've chanced another shot. I would have to keep my suspicions to myself a while longer. I certainly couldn't have Damian think he should go after the shooter. "My cell phone went into the water. Can I borrow yours?"

Damian looked at Pearlie disappearing around a bend. "To call the cops? I thought that's what Pearlie went to do."

"I need to get someone to bring out my air scent dog to track the shooter."

"Your dog can do that? That's cool, can I come too?" I still had to work out how to get him out of the way. This was not the time to tell him I thought his mother was a cold-blooded killer.

He reluctantly handed over his cell phone. "You're not going to call my Uncle Ian, are you? I'm supposed to be at the gym today."

"He'll need to come get you, but I'll explain that your CPR saved my life," I said, holding his cell phone to my ear. "There's no reception out here and I need to bring a blanket back for the body. Stay here and keep the curious away from the body until someone relieves you. Think you can do that?"

"Sure," he said, spreading his feet and crossing his arms over his chest.

"Good. By the way, have you seen your mom lately?"

"I haven't talked to my mother in a week or so. Why? Pearlie said that the man who had the gun on you was one of the suspects." Damian's main interest was on the murder case, not his mother.

"Yes, Wade Hamilton. He confessed to killing your father."

Damian stared down at the body. "Really? Then it's finally over. Uncle Ian and my mother will be glad to hear it."

I patted him on the shoulder. "Just promise me you'll stay here until you're relieved by a sheriff's deputy or the EMTs."

"Okay, but tell 'em to hurry. I'm not crazy about hanging out here with a dead body."

"I'll be back as soon as I can and trust me, Damian, he's not going anywhere."

Dead bodies aside, I would do just about anything to keep him away from the conversation I was going to have with Ian Tom about his sister. Knowing Damian, he would go ballistic and run off to try to find his mother, adding another innocent person to the mix.

There was only one problem with my plan. At the parking lot, Pearlie's Jeep door was open and her purse was on the driver's seat.

My heart rate spiked. No. No. Don't go there. She'll be back in a minute. Probably went to the bathroom. And leave her purse on the seat and the door unlocked? Damn!

I should've known better. Naomi was no fool. She'd backtracked to the parking lot and waited for one of us or all of us to show. She knew her son was with Pearlie. Was she hoping she could work some fairy tale on him to get his help? Or maybe she preferred one of us women, thinking we would be easy to intimidate. Even without her own weapon, my dimpled, chubby little cousin would be a handful, looking for a weakness, some way to get an advantage over her captor.

I looked up at the hills behind the lake. Wade may have been able to sneak into the showers at night and fish during the day, but he had to be sleeping somewhere close by. The rangers would check overnighters for their paid camping tags, so he couldn't stay in the park. He had to have someplace safe but near the lake, and if Naomi took off on foot it was because she knew about Wade's hidey-hole.

I used Damian's cell to make the 9-1-1 call that Pearlie obviously didn't get to make, then called Caleb and told him everything, including my theory that Naomi shot Wade Hamilton. "I only wish I'd confided my suspicions about Naomi to Pearlie before she was kidnapped. We'll need Hoover, so bring something of Pearlie's. No, wait. Bring Harley Aldrich too. Yes, I know what I'm saying."

Even with their sirens blazing a trail through traffic, we would have an hour's wait until they got here and I had Damian, aka the loose cannon, just itching to do something. This could go wrong in so many ways.

Chapter Twenty-eight:

I trotted back to where Damian stood guard over Wade Hamilton's body and after we covered it with the blanket, I turned to field questions from the crowd of fishermen and boaters. The minute I held up my hands for quiet, cell phones instantly appeared to video whatever gaff I might commit. I would have to remember to do the same the next time a law enforcement officer did something dumb.

"My name is Lalla Bains," I said, choosing my words carefully. "I'm a private investigator. The authorities have been called and they are on their way."

Questions punctured the air. I held up my hands again. "It is not my job to discuss this case with you. That will have to come from the sheriff's department and I sincerely doubt that you will hear anything else today. As a matter of fact, right now y'all are just in the way."

I felt a lump rise in my throat; dropping Pearlie's Texas drawl into my sentence made me even more fearful of the outcome. If cornered, I had no doubt that Naomi would use Pearlie as a human shield in order to escape. We had to find them and somehow talk Naomi into releasing Pearlie. I sincerely hoped Caleb was able to locate Harley. I suspected that before the day was over, we would need both dog and man.

Someone in the crowd said something about a siren and then I heard it. A deputy sheriff must've been in the area and was now responding to my 9-1-1 emergency. I reminded Damian against answering any questions, then told him it would probably be best if he just didn't talk at all, excused myself and trotted back to the parking lot.

Ian Tom was talking to the park ranger, but when he saw me he broke off and hurried over. "Lalla, are you all right?" he asked, taking me by the shoulders. "Your 9-1-1 call said someone had been shot."

"I'm fine, fine, but Wade Hamilton is dead."

Ian's expression told me he wasn't the least bit surprised. "I have deputies and the M.E. on the way. Can you tell me how it happened?"

"First, you need to tell me if your sister's car or truck is in this parking lot."

Ian's head snapped up. "Was she here? Have you seen her? What'd she say?"

"I haven't seen her, Ian, I just know that someone used a rifle, probably with a scope, to shoot Wade. And I think it was to keep him from telling us the truth about your sister's involvement in these murders. Now tell me, what does she drive and do you see it in this parking lot?"

His heavy sigh told me everything I needed to know. Until this minute, I suspected that Ian Tom might have been responsible for these recent murders. But now, I understood that his secret had more to do with his own suspicions about his sister.

"That's it, over there," he said, pointing to a Ford F150.

I nodded then said, "How'd you know I'd be here?"

"Your secretary told me where I might find you," he said.

"You suspected your sister but didn't consider sharing with us?"

"I didn't put it all together until today, okay?"

"Then fill me in while we wait for the troops."

"All right," he said with a heavy sigh. "You know I got phone taps on the suspects. Wade was getting calls from a burner cell. I couldn't trace the number, but today he got a two-minute call that pinged off a tower on top of the Dragoon Mountains. That's near enough to my sister's home for me to guess she was in contact with him and I knew this was the last place Wade Hamilton had been seen alive, so I decided to come out and try to find him, or her."

"What put you onto your sister in the first place?"

"I left Arizona as soon as I could, which in retrospect was a selfish thing to do because I left my younger sister in charge of our crazy dad. Don't get me wrong, I loved my father, but after Mom died, he went overboard with this shaman thing. So I didn't hear that Naomi was married and had a kid, or that her husband had been shot until I moved back here and got in touch with her. She and Damian were living out at our dad's place and she's got all this expensive jewelry making equipment. When I questioned how she could afford it all, she told me she had a benefactor, someone who wanted to see her happy. I figured I deserved the verbal slap and shut up about it. Then Damian graduated from high school and got work in Vegas as a welder, my wife got cancer and life went on. I didn't see or think about Naomi until Damian came back to train for American Ninja Warrior and he said his mother was paying for a P.I. I had to wonder why she wanted to dig up the past."

"And you thought by giving us three possible suspects, we'd hurry this along?" I asked.

"Actually, I was rather hoping I would be wrong. But when Jesse Jefferson was murdered with the same MO as Ron's, the blunt instrument to the back of the head, I got this itchy feeling that she was orchestrating all of it." He stopped to look at Naomi's truck. "She'll be hell to find if she's on foot."

"Why do you say that?"

"We're Chiricahua. My father taught both of us how to track and hide the Apache way."

"That well may be but Caleb is bringing trackers and here he comes."

Harley, unable to wait for Caleb's SUV to come to a stop, leaped out and ran over to me. "How long has she been gone?"

Harley's interest was zeroed in on one person only and that was Pearlie. I looked at my watch. "Half-an-hour?"

"We still have enough light, let's go," he said, shrugging into his daypack.

Caleb came around the side of the SUV and pulled me into a tight embrace. "Harley's up to speed on the problem and he seems to think he can find Pearlie even without your dog."

"But you brought Hoover, didn't you?" I asked. Harley might have a heightened sense of smell for a human, but nothing beats a trained air scent dog for tracking missing people.

Caleb stepped back and nodded for my dad to get out with the dog. He clipped the leash on Hoover and handed him over to me. I didn't have to tell Hoover that he was here to work. The dog's muscles quivered, his tail beat the ground, eyes on mine, waiting for the command to *search*. All I had to do was hold the cloth in front of his nose and say the word. But I handed the leash to my dad and told Harley to give us a minute.

Harley looked up at the sun heading toward the west. "A minute is all you'll get."

I patted Harley's tensed cheek and agreed to the necessity for speed, then dragged Caleb over to Ian. "Ian and I have been talking. I think Naomi shot Wade Hamilton."

Ian's eyes shuttered against the painful truth. "I didn't think it would go down like this, or so fast. I had my suspicions, but now..."

"Don't even think about backpedaling on your sister, Ian. She's taken my cousin Pearlie as a hostage," I said through clenched teeth. "So where would she go?"

Ian sucked in a quick breath and looked up at the mountains behind the lake. "We used to hike all over these mountains with our dad looking for petroglyphs and pot shards. If I remember right, there's a cave she could get to, but it's a hike. I see you brought your dog. Good thinking."

I motioned for Harley and my dad to join us. "Pearlie will do everything she can to slow down Naomi, but we have Hoover and Ian thinks he knows where she's going. Ian, Damian is standing guard over Wade's body. If you need to be there for your nephew, Caleb and I can take the dog and Harley to search for them."

Ian's jaw tightened with new resolution. "I'm going with you. I'll leave a couple of deputies to stay with my nephew until the M.E. gets here. It's starting to cloud up. We need to hurry if we want to get ahead of the rain."

If anyone had an alternative plan, I didn't hear it. I took Hoover's leash, signaled to Harley that we were ready, put the cloth in front of Hoover's nose and told him to search.

It took Hoover a few minutes to zigzag onto a trail, but when he found it, he surged forward, eager to find his lost people and get his reward.

An hour later, a strong breeze was blowing against us, bringing heavy dark clouds and a cooling effect on our hot skin. All the same, we halted every fifteen minutes to drink water. I poured out some from my bottle into a cup for Hoover, then straightened to look over the brown hills, the dry grass waving us forward.

"We should keep going," Ian said, glancing at the sky.

"We don't have Hoover's four-wheel drive," I said. Harley and I had on daypacks, but Ian and Caleb had to hike in flak-jackets and utility belts holstered sidearms, flashlights and handcuffs.

"I'm good," Harley said. "Hoover and I can find her."

"Sorry, pal," Ian said, "but I'm going with you."

"Me too," Caleb said, adjusting his utility belt.

Harley doffed his hat and bowed. "Then after you, sirs."

"Ian, if it rains, could you still find the cave?" I asked.

"I don't know," he said. "I haven't been here in years."

"Then let's not waste any more time," I said, encouraging Hoover to keep moving.

Forty minutes later, we were well into the foothills and that much closer to the mountains and a cave. The good news was that the wind had abated; the bad news was that lightning was now powering through a huge black cloud and it was moving this way.

"Oh great. Now we have lightning strikes to worry about," I muttered.

Caleb put his arm around me. "We're almost to the mountains. We'll find shelter soon."

"It better be soon," I said, "I just felt a raindrop on my nose."

I was hot, tired and footsore, and except for Hoover and Harley, I was sure the others were feeling the same. I handed Harley the leash.

"Are you sure?" he asked.

"We're all but worn out and you're not even winded, but if you find the cave and Pearlie's inside, don't do anything. Just use your cell and call one of us. Promise?"

He accepted Hoover's leash and striding away, soon outdistanced us.

We continued to follow, but kept our pace reasonable so as not to completely exhaust ourselves. As water laden clouds started covering the sky, thunder rolled overhead and I jumped at the crack of lightning.

Another lit up the sky, and Ian stopped so suddenly that I bumped into him. "There!" he said, pointing. "That lightning strike lit up the entrance to the cave. That's where she's gone. I know it."

"Then we should take a more indirect approach," Caleb said.

Just then, another sound exploded through the air, but this time, I knew it wasn't thunder. I froze, then took off running.

"Lalla! Wait up," Caleb called after me.

"She's shooting at Harley and Hoover," I yelled over my shoulder and kept running.

To make myself a smaller target, I ran the twenty or so yards in a crouch and threw myself onto the ground next to them. Hoover wagged a hello and Harley grunted and pointed to the cave.

"Are either of you hurt?" I asked, breathlessly.

"She's not *that* good of a shot," Harley said. "While one of you distracts her, I'll crawl up those rocks behind the cave. Unless you or the sheriff got another plan?"

"Not yet, but the guys are right behind me," I said, stretching my neck to peer over the top of the weeds.

I felt another shot whizz past my ear and dropped to the ground, my heart in my throat. "Dammit! That was close!"

"Like a she-wolf," Harley said. "She's got her back to the wall with no way out."

Caleb and Ian flopped down beside us.

Caleb grabbed my arm. "You're going back."

"No. I'm not leaving, not with Pearlie in there."

"Told you she wouldn't go," Ian said.

"Since it looks like she's eager to shoot at anything that moves, Harley wants to get up on the rocks behind her."

"Alright then," Ian said. "We'll split up. Lalla and Caleb will go to one side and I'll take the other. I'll try to talk her out before she does any more damage."

No one could argue with Ian's plan; it was his sister.

Caleb and I took Hoover and crawled through the weeds to the right. Ian and Harley went to the left where Harley started climbing the rocks above the cave.

"Do you think Ian will be able to talk her into giving up?"

"He'll try," he said, un-holstering his weapon.

I put my hand on his. "Caleb, you can't get a clean shot from this far away. Besides, she'll use Pearlie as a shield."

"Few people can accurately shoot a rifle while holding onto a hostage," he said. "And you said so yourself; Pearlie will do everything she can to resist. We're counting on it now. I'll only shoot if I have to."

I ground my teeth in frustration. "You're betting my cousin's life against a mad-woman!"

I was still thinking about the logistics of this risky venture when Ian stepped out in front of the cave, his hands in the air. The wind blew away his words, but Naomi did as he and Caleb guessed. She had Pearlie by the neck, bound and gagged and she had her rifle to my cousin's head.

Lightning flashed and thunder boomed across the mountains.

I was so mad at that point I would've rushed her myself, but it started to rain and then fell in sheets so thick that wiping the water away from our eyes did nothing and Ian and Naomi disappeared behind the curtain of water.

A voice shouted and the dull sound of another shot was the response. I didn't wait for permission and sprinted ahead, Caleb pounding after me.

Harley stood at the mouth of the cave, clutching Pearlie to his chest. Ian stood over a writhing Naomi, his gun in his hand. He reached down and hauled her up over his shoulder and carried her into the shelter of the cave.

The cave had probably been used by animals long before Wade's unwashed clothes took over and I wrinkled my nose against the smell of mildew and old cooking grease.

Ian lowered Naomi onto a dirty sleeping bag and examined her shoulder wound. Her eyes were closed and the long gray braid had come undone, wet strands of hair draped like seaweed across her face. For a moment, I was underwater again, looking at a woman who had already drowned.

Shaking off the macabre image, I grabbed one of Wade's dirty shirts and gave it to Ian to stanch the blood oozing from her wound.

Taking another shirt, Ian ripped it into strips, padded the wound with one piece and wrapped a long strip around her shoulder, making a sling for her arm. Naomi remained unconscious throughout the entire ordeal and I saw for the first time the lines bracketing her face, the ones that had developed over the years as she schemed and planned to get what she thought she deserved.

I got to my feet and laid a hand on Ian's shoulder. "Can we talk for a minute?"

Ian slowly dragged himself to his feet, gave his pale-faced sister one last worried look and then joined my dad, Caleb, Harley and Pearlie.

I went to Pearlie, still wrapped in Harley's arms and asked, "Did she say anything to you?"

Pearlie started to speak, then frowned at Harley's grip on her. "Thanks, Harley, but I can stand on my own now. The only thing she said to me was, 'Move!' And every time I thought to slow down, she'd poke me with her rifle."

I nodded. "She could've left in her truck with no one the wiser. Instead she chose to take a hostage and retrace Wade's path to this place. Why?"

Ian said, "She must've set him up here with supplies and a sleeping bag and I suppose it was so she could keep tabs on him."

"I guess so. She shot him in front of her own son, so she must've wanted him dead. But again, why not leave? Why come back here?"

Pearlie piped up. "She tied me up and gagged me so I'd stay put, then went tearing into stuff. I think she was lookin' for sumpthin'."

"Her call to Wade," I said. "Ian, you said it lasted only two minutes. Whatever she said must've spooked him. He was in a real hurry when he saw me. If he hadn't stopped to intercept me, he might've gotten away."

Caleb took out his flashlight and raked the light across the damp walls. "That rock in the wall over there sticks out."

We moved as one to see what Caleb would find. He pulled at the rock, but when it wouldn't budge, Ian took his knife and wedged it out.

At a scuffling sound we all turned to see Naomi jump to her feet, run out of the cave and disappear. A few pebbles rolled down into the cave and Ian shook his head in disbelief. "She's gone up!"

"What do you mean?" I said, furious that we'd been so easily fooled.

"Never mind. She's weak, she can't get far. I'll go," Ian said.

Weak? Even now, Ian was still making excuses for her. We followed him out into the clearing sky and watched as he nimbly climbed.

Above him, Naomi looked back, shouted at him and kept going.

Ian didn't waste any breath replying, he just kept climbing over wet and slippery rocks.

When they dipped out of sight, we moved out further from under the protection of the overhanging rocks. "There!" Pearlie said pointing. "I can see her. She's coming down."

"Thank God!" I said.

Naomi stopped and looked back to where her brother was picking his way over the rocks after her. She tried to lift her arm, but her injury must've hurt too much. Injured and bitterly angry that her plan was about to be thwarted, she scrambled over the last few rocks until she was standing on the edge of a boulder. With her body outlined against a clearing sky, she lifted her voice in a plaintive song.

I felt a shaky moment of déjà vu and shivered in the cooling air. But this time it wasn't a song from Bible school, it was something in her native tongue. As her voice rose in strength, it echoed across the mountains, and for a moment, I thought I heard the accompaniment of the old man's drum.

Ian, stumbling to get to her, called out, "No! Naomi, don't!"

Instead of responding, she simply blew him a kiss and leaped to her death.

Chapter Twenty-nine:

Pearlie found Wade's confession behind a loose rock in the cave. He blamed Naomi for everything. From manipulating him into murdering Naomi's husband, Pastor Jesse and Ron Barbour to his smelly socks and the lousy canned food she'd stocked the cave with. Typical of Wade and Naomi—it was always someone else's fault.

The helicopter arrived, but Ian stayed only long enough to see Naomi's body aboard and then insisted on returning with us so that he could talk privately to Damian. We silently walked single file through the wet grass, water squishing out of our shoes, bodies too tired to think of anything other than getting clean and dry again.

When we hit the parking lot, Ian asked to speak to us. "I have to take some responsibility for precipitating my sister's murderous actions. If Wade Hamilton said he was running from Naomi, it was because he finally understood that he was as expendable as Ron Barbour and Jesse Jefferson."

"You also put Andy Sokolov on that list," I said. "And while I don't know how we could ever prove he tried to blow us up in my dad's mine, I take it you wanted someone else to dig up his sordid past?"

"Yes. I couldn't prove Andy was a child molester without looking like I was trying to ruin the mayor's reputation. But thanks to Caleb's help, Andy was arrested last night. He was caught in a sting when he tried to hook up with a

Sacramento woman who could pass for a sixteen-year-old. At the very least, his prison sentence will keep him away from young girls for the rest of his life."

"What're you going to tell Damian?" I asked.

"It will take some time for him to sort it all out, but I've decided to take a leave of absence so I can drive him to the try-outs for America Ninja Warrior. If he doesn't get in at one city, we'll drive to the next try-out. I'm hoping it will give us both the time we need to heal."

~~~~~~~~~~

I slept long and hard that night, waking only when coffee was waved under my nose. "What time is it?"

"Ten a.m." Caleb said, handing me the mug.

I blew on the hot coffee and looked him over. "Aren't you a bit late for work?"

"I've been to the office and back. Your dad is here and wants to talk to us."

I put the coffee on the bedside table and my feet on the floor, worry jolting me awake. "What is it? Is someone hurt?"

"Not yet," he said, with a grin. "The Garza boys hitched a ride home, but since no one was there, they came to the police station to turn themselves in."

"They did what? Wait, how did they...?"

"They were hungry and remembered that we fed them before taking them up to the reservation, so they figured I was good for at least one more run to McDonald's. I got them their burgers, put them in a cell and called their social worker. She's trying to find them a place, but in the meantime, I brought them out here."

"Here? What happened to the folks at the reservation?"

"Well that's why your dad is here. They sort of wore out their welcome."

"What'd they do?" I asked, putting my bare feet into slippers and pulling on a robe.

"They set the barn on fire—with the two older brothers in it."

"My God! Was anyone hurt?"

"A couple of backsides got tanned, which only seems fair."

I remembered the teenaged boys and their clear dislike of the newcomers. "I suppose they had good reason."

Caleb said, "They threatened to run away again if they couldn't stay in Wishbone."

"They didn't last a whole week," I said.

"I know," he said, motioning me to follow him into the living room.

My father smiled nervously.

"No! You can't be serious. Dad," I said, pulling him outside. "What're you thinking? They're a couple of hellions."

"Excuse me, but I raised you and your brother by myself, didn't I? I'm retired now with plenty of time on my hands, and it's only for a month until their mother gets out of rehab."

"A lot can happen with these kids in a month," I said. "They tried to burn down a barn with people in it. What if they try to do the same to you?"

"I haven't got a barn. Besides, they have their own room with two separate beds, and when they're not in school I'll keep them busy."

I thought he had lost his mind, but if he was willing to be responsible for them, who was I to argue, so I didn't.

Seeing we'd reached an agreement, the boys happily wrapped their arms around my dad.

"We'll be good," the younger one said, looking up at him with big brown puppy eyes.

"And we'll clean and cook for you," the older one added.

"That won't be necessary," Dad said. "I have a housekeeper and she'll prepare our meals, but you'll have chores to do."

I almost laughed. Coco Lucero hadn't been crazy about the dog as a live in, what she was going to think of two little boys?

"You got any horses? You got a TV? The other family didn't even have a TV."

"I have a TV and a dog."

"Oh, good," the older one said. "Will you take us to the baseball games in Wishbone? Our brother plays for the Red Sox and we always go to the games."

"Sure," my dad said, running a shaky hand through his wispy hair. "I like baseball."

I laughed. "Okay, you have my blessing, Dad. Just don't ask me to babysit."

The boys turned solemn faces to me. "We don't need babysitting. We're going to be real good, and it's only until our mom gets out of rehab."

Feeling sorry I said anything, I asked, "Have you boys had breakfast?"

"I'm still hungry," the little one said.

"We had a breakfast sandwich at McDonald's," The older one said. "But that was hours ago. Whadya got?"

"Bacon and eggs coming up," I said, and left them with Caleb and Dad while I fixed it.

We were finishing up breakfast when I got a call from Pearlie. "You need to get over here, *now.*"

"By *here*, I suppose you mean the office. Why? Has the state closed us down already?"

"The office. Now. And make it snappy."

I hung up, my earlier good mood gone up in smoke.

"Trouble?" Caleb asked. "You go on, I'll clean up."

Distracted, I nodded my thanks, dressed in a hurry and ran for the Jeep.

Taking the stairs two at a time, I threw open the door to our office and gasped.

Papers were scattered on the floor, our resident skeleton was toppled, and all of the file cabinets had been pushed away from the wall.

The first thing I thought of was that we'd been robbed, but Damian was with Ian and they were on their way to the American Ninja try-outs, Wade and Naomi were dead, and Andy Sokolov was in jail awaiting trial.

Pearlie sat with her hands folded over some papers. "Have a seat," she said.

"Where're the twins?" I asked. "Have they seen this mess? Have you called the police?"

"No need to call the cops and the twins made the mess. Here's their letter," she said, handing me the single sheet from an envelope.

It said,

It's been fun, but you didn't think we were here 'cause we love answering phones, did you? We found his stash and we know you girls will appreciate how we did it. His birthday is April 4th, 1944. We looked in the fourth file cabinet from the left. The forty-fourth file from the front and there was the key taped to the file. Then we looked for the safe. His house was demolished and we know that Pearlie kept the bank statements, so we nixed the idea of a safety deposit box. Sorry, ladies, but we always knew we had to think like Ron—the low-down skunk. As you can see, we found the safe behind the file cabinet. We had the key and all we had to do was figure out the combination. The combination was 04-04-44. That man never could keep a secret from us.

I looked up at Pearlie and sighed. "It would've been nice if they'd left us a few bucks."

"They paid our rent for next month," she said, handing me the payment slip. "In cash, of course. And we have one other bonus."

My eyes were glued on the business-sized envelope in her hands. "Have you read it?"

"Yeah," she said, pushing it over to me. "Open it."

Dear Lalla and Pearlie, If you are reading this then I'm gone, or dead and you two got smart and figured out where I put my safe, or my exes did it for you.

If you were stupid enough to leave them alone in my office for any amount of time, then you can forget about the hundred grand I had in the safe. Though I suppose filthy lucre isn't your thing. You girls never did understand what it takes to be successful. The twins don't have any such scruples. Those girls have always been too smart for their own good. They're also an irresistible combination of insatiable greed and unprincipled ambi-

tion, which is why I loved them long enough to marry them.

Well ladies, I taught you everything I know and if you're still determined to become P.I's, I guess you deserve the chance. It's the least, and the last thing, I can do for you. Bon voyage, amigas.
Ron

The next two pages were letters of recommendation for each of us as private investigators to Arizona's State Board of Licenses.

The End

If you enjoyed this 5th book in the Dead Red Mystery series as much as I enjoyed writing it, I hope that you'll consider leaving a favorable review on Amazon

There are 4 more in the Dead Red Mystery Series, starting with:

#1-A DEAD RED CADILLAC

Twice-divorced NY model Lalla Bains now runs her dad's crop-dusting business in Modesto, California, where she's hoping to dodge the inevitable fortieth birthday party. But when her trophy red vintage Caddy is found tail fins up in a nearby lake, the police ask why a widowed piano teacher, who couldn't possibly see beyond the hood ornament, was found strapped in the driver's seat.

Reeling from an interrogation with local homicide, Lalla is determined to extricate herself as a suspect in this strange murder case. Unfortunately, drug-running pilots, a cross-dressing convict, a crazy Chihuahua, and the dead woman's hunky nephew throw enough roadblocks to keep Lalla neck-deep in an investigation that links her family to a twenty-year-old murder only she can solve.

~~~~~~~~~~

#2-A DEAD RED HEART

What would you do if the love of your life lost their chance for a heart transplant because the donor organ went to a convicted felon? Grieve and let go? Or wait for your chance at justice and revenge?

When a homeless Vet litters her beloved red Cadillac with poetry scrawled on paper snowflakes, Lalla decides to confront him. But that doesn't mean she wants the man to drop dead at her feet—with a pair of blue handled scissors sticking out of his chest. With nothing but the man's last words for the police to go on, Lalla decides that someone needs to be on the side of this misunderstood vet, and that person will be the exasperating, pushy, tenacious, Ms. Lalla Bains. But digging into the man's past will only unravel a more potent question: What would you do if the love of your life lost their chance for a heart transplant because the donor organ went to a convicted felon?

~~~~~~~

#3- A DEAD RED OLEANDER

Full time ag-pilot and part time crime sleuth, Lalla Bains, is juggling end of season work with the arrival quirky Texas relatives and a greenhorn pilot.

Satisfied that the pilot is legit and that her relatives can resist putting her dad's pet goat on the dinner menu, Lalla gets back to business.

But things go south in a hurry when the pilot drops dead and his tearful widow is accused of poisoning her husband. Now Lalla's got to sort out why a U.S. Marshal and a shadowy Las Vegas hit man are suddenly so interested in this pilot and his wife.

~~~~~~~

#4-A DEAD RED ALIBI

A successful, but reclusive young artist with a secret life that will turn deadly.

A wannabe lawman and his dotty gun-toting granddad.

An abandoned mine pit, a curious dad and the local police chief found with him.

When Lalla and her dad take a trip to Arizona to inspect her new property, Dad disappears. But when Lalla enlists the help of a local tracker she's relieved to find him un-harmed, in the bottom of a mine pit and he's got company—a local police chief, and it looks like he's been murdered. Then too, a young woman artist living nearby has also been murdered. What're the chances that these two murders are going to be related? Well, if you're Lalla Bains, you don't guess, you start looking for the killer!

~~~~~~~

#6: A DEAD RED GAMBLE: Coming January 2016

*Get the 1st three complete novels as a boxed set on Kin-dle: http://getBook.at/B00GY8W5D2

U.S. and International readers can find more of the Dead Red Series at MY AMAZON AUTHOR PAGE: http://www.amazon.com/RPDahlke/e/B004S2NJFO/

About the Author

I sort of fell into the job of running a crop-dusting business when my dad decided he'd rather go on a cruise than take another season of lazy pilots, missing flaggers, testy farmers and horrific hours. After two years at the helm, I handed him back the keys and fled to a city without any of the above. And no, I was never a crop-duster.

I write about a tall, blond and beautiful ex-model turned crop-duster who, to quote Lalla Bains, says: "I've been married so many times they oughta revoke my license." I wanted to give readers a peek at the not so-perfect -life of a beautiful blond. Lalla Bains is no Danielle Steele character, she's not afraid of chipping her manicure. Scratch that, the girl doesn't have time for a manicure what with herding a bunch of recalcitrant pilots and juggling work orders just to keep her father's flagging business alive.

Other books on Kindle by RP Dahlke:

A romantic sailing mystery trilogy:
A Dangerous Harbor http://getBook.at/B0062D4GM2
Hurricane Hole http://viewBook.at/B00FT1EI1C
Coming next in the trilogy – Dead Rise

~~~~

Jump Start Your Book Promotions
http://viewBook.at/B00HZ2RM70

You can reach RP Dahlke at her website:
http://rpdahlke.com
or e-mail: rp@rpdahlke.com

or at my AMAZON AUTHOR PAGE:
http://www.amazon.com/RP-Dahlke/e/B004S2NJFO/

Facebook: http://facebook.com/rpdahlke

GoodReads:
https://www.goodreads.com/book/show/18664399-
hurricane-hole

Sign up to get my infrequent newsletter or to get in on
Raffles and free goodies at my website & blog:
http://rpdahlke.com